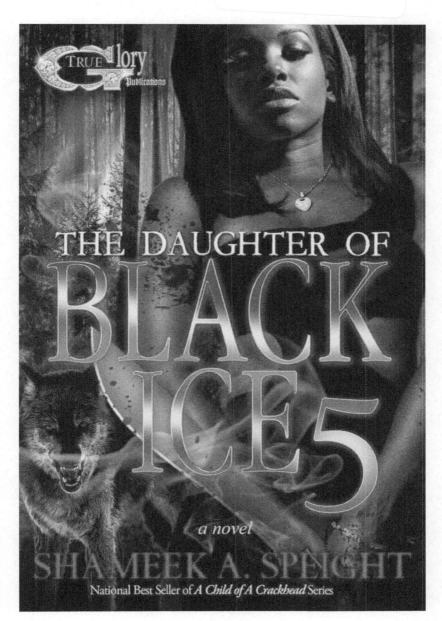

THE DAUGHTER OF
BLACK ICE 5

a novel

SHAMEEK A. SPEIGHT

National Best Seller of *A Child of A Crackhead* Series

DAUGHTER OF BLACK ICE 5.

SHAMEEK SPEIGHT.

ACKNOWLEDGMENTS

I want to say thank you to all the people that have supported my books all these years, and to my new readers, welcome to my sick mind; I hope you have fun. Lol, but if you're looking for an everyday type of story full of love and romance with happy endings, you won't get that here.

My goal is to live up to my name, the king of urban horror, to be one of the greatest storytellers and writers that ever lived, to draw you into a story that you can see in your mind, to have you shocked and say "Oh shit!" but want to keep reading more. My books and stories are one of a kind and will take you to a place you've never been before. There's only one Shameek A. Speight, one king of urban horror. I created my lane and will do my best to take it to another level. You're about to enter my world, and I hope you enjoy it.

Please leave reviews on Amazon, and feel free to reach out to me and share your experience of reading one of my novels. Your support is greatly appreciated. God bless. I hope you enjoy this book if you're new to my work. To learn more about certain characters like Michael, read A Child of a crackhead series 1-6; to learn about Faith, read Daughter of Black ice 1-5. To learn about Zaira read, I couldn't hear her scream 1-3. All my novels are connected.

Thank you for the love and support.

TABLE OF CONTENTS

SYPNOSIS

Faith learned that her bloodline runs deeper than she thought and why her family is evil.

She is a child of the Devil himself; with this newfound knowledge, she must figure out how to use it to save her children and kill someone she once would have died for.

While trying to convince her brother, Michael, she's nothing like their father, Black ice before it's too late.

CHAPTER 1

"What the fuck!" Janice said as she rushed upstairs to the blood bath.

Michael was coughing up blood, trying to hold on to his life as blood poured out his chest. Zaira was sitting down with her legs crossed Indian style next to Envy, who was lying on her side trying to breathe and bleeding out.

Zaira had a huge evil grin as she poked Envy with the ice pick. Not deep, just deep enough to make the tip enter Envy's body and leave a small perfect hole. Janice grabs Zaira's hand.

"What's wrong with you? She's family," Janice said, making sure Zaira could read her lips.

"So! Sometimes family can be your worst enemy," Zaira said, snatching her hand free from Janice and standing up.

She was short, around 4'9". She looked up at Janice.

"You're family, so keep that in mind," Zaira said and walked off.

"Did that little bitch just threaten me?" Janice asked as she couldn't believe her ears.

"What happened here? Was it Black ice? I saw him walk out the front door; where had he been?" Janice asked.

"No, this was me; I don't know what happened; I was in a trance; it was that damn book I was reading. I need you to get the formula from the henchmen down the block; call them fast; hurry!" Faith said as her heart raced.

Janice pulled out her phone and texted the henchmen.

Three of them met her at the front door with a small suitcase. She took it upstairs and opened it. Inside was two syringes. She passed one to

Faith and poked the tip of the needle into the one she had in Envy's neck.

"Uhmm, are you sure you want to do this? I'm not saying we should let them die or anything like that. I'm saying that you just stabbed your brother and took his eyes and tongue," Janice stated.

"Yes, I want to do this. What are you trying to say?" Faith said.

"I'm saying they're going to be very pissed off. If you know what I mean." Janice replied.

"Just do it before they die." Faith shouted and jammed the needle in Michael's neck and pushed the liquid formula Inside him, and Janice did the same for Envy.

Envy starts coughing uncontrollably.

"Uhmm, is she supposed to do that?" Janice asked, and Faith shrugged. Then looked down at Michael.

"Is it working? It usually doesn't take this long."

"*Ughh!*" Envy gasped for air, then sat up while breathing in and out deeply.

"*I guess it's slower than the one that is in me. I start healing in five or ten minutes. You and black ice, that Red velvet chick, and that demon child you call your sister were instant. I'm telling you, Faith, something isn't right with her,*" Janice said.

"*Now isn't the time to discuss this,*" Faith said while worrying and wondering why Michael's body took so long to start healing.

"*Why isn't it working? Wake up! Get up!*" Faith shouted.

"*If the brain to badly damaged, the formula doesn't work; we don't know about it so much,*" Janice said.

"*That is not true. Zaira's face was blown halfway off, her friends betrayed her, and I gave her my blood, and she was okay. She healed, and I think she was dead. This should still work. Black ice said only if your head is chopped off. There is no coming back from that,"* Faith said.

"That is not true. He came back," Michael said as his tongue and eyes slowly started to grow back.

"Years ago, he stole a clone machine from a secret military base and cloned himself. That is not even my birth father, just a copy of him. The real one I killed two years ago," Michael mumbled, and Faith sat him up and hugged him tightly.

"I'm sorry! I'm sorry! I didn't mean to. Something came over me. That wasn't me. I wasn't in control of myself. It was the books. Josephine Journal. I was there," Faith said as she hugged him harder.

"Clone machine, what in the Government conspiracy. Cloning is not real; it can't be," Janice said, not believing her ears.

"If it's not real, why is it against the law to clone a person or try to? We can clone plants in our own house. I have done it, and they have been

cloning animals for meat longer than I have been alive. Somehow, my father figured this out, killed everyone on a small military base, and took the machine. I didn't know this until I read one of his journals. I just thought he came back from the dead. But the new him was younger and had all his memories, the perfect copy of him. Then he got some type of formula from one of the Teflon divas that made him able to heal instantly and made him stronger and faster, so this Black ice is harder to kill," Michael said.

"Bitch get your hands off my husband after you pretty much killed him. How dare you, you're hugging him." Envy shouted, and Faith broke her embrace.

"See, I liked you, but your sister just poked me up like a Mexican in jail, smiling the whole time; she was doing it and having fun. There is something seriously wrong with that little heifer. I swear to God I'm going blow her smiling ass head off her shoulders.

I knew something was wrong when she walked around with a jar full of bugs. What kind of girl play with bugs, and how come I'm not fucking hurt no more." Envy shouted.

 "*It's not her fault, Envy; it's mine. I tried to kill her while she was sleeping.*" Michael stated.

"*Huh? You try to do what? You are telling me you tried to kill your sister, and I got stabbed because she ended up beating your ass,*" Envy said.

"*Yes, I kept feeling sick, like something was wrong; I thought it was the books; they released some kind of dark energy, and I kept feeling that my father was here and close. His dark aura and thought it was coming off Faith, but I was wrong; she was just defending herself. It was that book and the fact my father was here.*" Michael stated.

"*It's worse than that. I don't know how to explain, but Black ice wasn't supposed to get his hands on those books. I saw how our family came to be; Josephine, our ancestor, made a deal with the devil by using those books, all this time, you thought our father was the devil, but he was just the Devil's child. The real fucking devil was Josephine's children's father, she's the devil's baby mama, and we're the results of that,"* Faith said.

"Did you learn all that by reading that book?" Janice asked.

"You're not understanding. It's deeper than that. I was there; I was in Josephine's body, felt everything, tasted everything. She made the deal to kill her master, her father, who was raping her but shit, none of that matters right now.

An old lady could see me inside Josephine; she talked directly to me, called my name, and said, don't let Black ice get his hands in the books again. It meant something terrible," Faith said.

" You were smoking some of that good-ass weed, the devil, and you were trapped inside your ancestors' body back in the time of slavery," Janice said and pulled out a blunt filled with weed and lit it up.

"After all the shit you have seen and been through, you find that part hard to believe, like really, bitch we were buried alive under concrete walls, and look how we met and who my father is. Yeah, this shit is far from normal, but it's real. All of it, and we can't just escape it." Faith replied.

"Speaking of bitch, I'm sorry Michael and Faith, but I'm fucking going to kill all of you little sister; it's seriously something mentally off with her. As I was dying, that little bitch kept poking me and smiling." Envy stated.

"Uhmm, you should let us deal with her," Michael said, then looked at Faith, knowing she could do things they couldn't.

Faith could beat her, but Faith knew it would get more difficult as she got older and wiser.

CHAPTER 2

Egypt's growling could be heard. Faith stood up and ran to the stairs with Michael and Envy behind her.

At the first door, getting ready to leave, was Black ice with a black duffel bag full of something. He turned around and looked at his children.

"You should have let him die, Faith. I warned you about being too soft, and this will be the third time. You are faster and stronger than any of my other children and ruthless; I trained you well.

You're a far cry from that helpless girl I found you as, but you still won't let go," Black ice said in a dark demonic tone.

His presence made everyone in the house scared. They all had a history of him trying to kill them, even Envy.

"Let what go?" Faith said.

"Your humanity, we're not like everyone else; we never will. To pretend is lying to yourself, hurting yourself. All we want to do is kill and make others feel pain. It's who we are, children. To deny it Is to deny your strength.

You should have let your brother and his bitch of a wife die. You keep picking the wrong people to love; love your pets and those that will bleed for you. That is it, my children.

I thought you'll be the one to replace me, to carry on my work. I thought you were the one, but you're not. I now know who it is," Black ice said, and Zaira stepped out of the shadows smiling and stood by his side.

Faith's eyes open wide, and she starts talking with her fingers in sign language.

"What are you doing? You're my sister. I need you; don't do anything foolish," Faith said.

"You had your time with him; he trained you and taught you a lot; it's my turn to learn from my father, my turn to see what it is like to have a Dad and understand more about the urge I have to kill, I'm going with him. You can't understand how I feel. He was in your life. You had him," Zaira said back in sign language.

"I understand; he didn't come into my life until I was eighteen; I never had a father until then, so I understand you want and need him, but it's not what you think. His love is cold, I can't stop you, but I need you, sister. I need you to help me get my children back. They outnumber us ten to one. I can't do this without help; please help me." Faith said and tried not to cry.

She knew she needed Zaira's help and hoped their shared love as siblings would be enough.

"Please, sister—" Faith plead.

Zaira looked at her.

13

"You had your turn. Now I'm sorry, but I got to put myself first," Zaira said in sign language back.

"Enough of this, let's go!" Black ice said, not revealing he knew sign language and understood everything they had said.

He started learning it when Zaira was born and has watched her since then. Like all of his children. He was never too far from them or had henchmen close by to give him an update.

Faith Jumped down the stairs and got in a fighting stance.

"You're not going anywhere with the books; leave them here." Faith shouted.

Black ice turned back around. His dark skin complexion seemed to shine; he was handsome but scary. He smiled, showing his perfect white teeth, and looked at her with a demonic look.

"You think you're ready to take me, little one. You're good, but I don't think you have it. You

have a lot of me in you, unlike your two brothers. But you keep thinking this fantasy of trusting people and loving them that they won't cross you.

Your brother will try to kill you again, it's what he does, and your men and henchmen betrayed you because you show them, love.

They wouldn't dare do that to me. Your children are in the compound in Alaska. So the henchmen with Lefty told me. See, they fear me.

I am the bogeyman, the Devil in the flesh. They wouldn't harm my blood without my say, but I want to see how this plays out.

See what you are, my daughter. You were my favorite, and you still are, show me why I feel this way." Black ice said.

When he called her his favorite, Zaira read his lips, and his face tightened up.

I'll be your favorite; I'll show you. Zaira thought to herself.

Envy came down the stairs with the short pump shotgun and, without saying a word, squeezed the trigger and shot Zaira in the chest. The impact of the shotgun pellets lifted Zaira off her feet and slammed her into the front door frame. But her bulletproof suit made the pellets bounce off and not penetrate. So Envy aimed and squeezed the trigger a second time. Black ice spun as the bullets hit his bulletproof leather pea coat.

"Die! Just fucking die. You got damn candy, man. You always have on that damn coat even in the summer;" Envy shouted as Black ice moved toward her fast.

She jumped back as he swung at her. She could feel herself moving faster than before.

This is what it's like to be them. Envy thought to herself as her heart raced, and it seemed as everyone else was moving in slow motion.

"You get away from her!" Michael shouted as he jumped down the stairs with his dagger.

No shirt on, just pajama pants.

"Fucking dramatic, all of you are fucking dramatic and wonder why I try to kill you; all of you are slow as pudding. Worse than the victims that be screaming, why me! Help me, someone help me, knowing damn well no one is coming to save them. As yours if I'm here to kill you, who can save you?" Black ice said sarcastically.

"I don't need anyone to save me; I killed you before and can do it again." Michael shouted and started swinging at Black ice.

Black ice dodged his blows with ease and laughed. Then pulled out one of his machetes from his thigh hostler and blocked Michael's attacks.

The sound of metal hitting against each other echoes throughout the house. Black ice punched Michael in the lip; then front kicked him in the stomach. Michael slid back and groaned in pain, holding his stomach.

"Do you think you beat me? I allow you and your brother to kill that old version of me, to get the government off my back. I kidnapped an influential person's daughter.

What's ironic is that the government now works with me and sanctions what I do. As long as I'm not sloppy and kill many of their elite, rich white folks, they turned their heads and paid me millions for human trafficking. They call it population control. How do you think I can get away with the things I've been doing for years. They don't want the world to know there's a black serial killer, that there is someone out there more intelligent than them and more dangerous.

You fight so hard to be the good guy, son, but there is no good guy. The same system you are trying to protect, act as if I don't exist and know I do." Black ice said, then smiled his evil grin and started laughing.

His laughter sent chills down everyone's spine in the house.

"You lie! You're a fucking goddamn liar. You didn't let me beat you. I won that fight." Michael shouted as his pride and ego got the best of him.

"It wasn't even you that won it. It was Mike. See, I learned that you and your older brother Bless are strong killers, but gene does matter. All of your mother DNA was strong and too much in both of you, unlike Mike or Faith over there or Zaira. They may have a chance of beating me one day, but I doubt it." Black ice said, then laughed. Then stop short and look him dead in the eyes.

His eyes were cold; you could see he was a murderer and killer. It was written all over him; there was no hiding what he was.

"Let me repeat; you can never! Never in your life beat me, son. I mess up with you; you're self-taught. Only know twenty percent of what I know from fighting me; unlike Faith, who I trained, you can't even beat your baby sisters.

How can you expect to stop me? Just stop this and join me. There are others we have to kill; you read my Journal. All of you have cousins out there. I have an older daughter out there. We need to find and kill that side of the bloodline before they come for us. I need to kill my twin sister," Black ice said.

"Fuck you! I'll never be like you!" Michael shouted.

"I know you can't; you're too fucking weak. But you, Faith, nothing can stop you. If you stop once, stop giving love, and expect it in return, too much love will get you hurt—you are still my favorite." Black ice said and looked her dead in her eyes.

Faith knew deep down in his sick twisted way he loved her; he loved them all but couldn't expect weakness.

Zaira read his lips once more of him calling Faith his favorite and couldn't control herself.

"Ahhhh!" She screamed, and a loud buzzing sound could be heard. Then she looked at Faith as if she wanted to fight.

"Don't you do this, Zaira! Don't you fucking dare! I need you," Faith said as she tried to plead with her but knew it was too late.

Thousands of black flies bust through the house's front and back windows.

"Not this again!" Janice said and pouted.

"Your sister is nasty; I did tell you that, right? Just fucking nasty and freak me out. If you weren't my best friend right now, I'd say fuck it and run. I can deal with the man-eating hyenas, wolves, all the death I got used to and became numb to but bugs! Fucking insects is where I'm drawing a line."

Janice closed her mouth and tightened her lips shut after having a flashback to when she first met Zaira and made flies travel down her throat.

The thought of it made Janice want to vomit, but she did her best to hold it in.

In a matter of seconds, the house was full of black flies. They were making it almost impossible to see and hear as they started biting Envy, Michael, and Janice, but not Faith. The fly seemed to run away from her.

"How are you doing this? You don't have your suit on," Zaira said, remembering when she fought Faith, and the insects wouldn't attack her.

Faith said she had a special bug repellent in her suit. She had made it when she discovered Zaira's gift.

"Are you doing this, Zaira? You're pissing me off, little sister! I'm mean, pissing me off." Faith said as she got angry.

Zaira tries her hardest to tell the flies to attack her as well as Faith walked down the stairs slowly holding the rail, dressed in a blue nightgown.

How is she doing this without her suit? I don't understand.

"Maybe you need to go with your father because you still haven't learned the lesson I taught. Don't show your hands, not even to family. Black ice number one rule; the reason I'm his favorite is because I listened and adapted." Faith said, knowing Zaira could read her lips.

"Ahhhh!" Zaira screamed and attacked. She pulled out a knife and threw it at Faith's face.

She easily caught it and used it to block the second knife Zaira threw at her chest.

"This is pointless," Faith said. But she had forgotten how fast and short Zaira was.

Zaira ran up to her and kicked her legs while still walking down the stairs. Fault tumbled down a few stairs and got up on her knees as Zaira poked her in the chest with an ice pick.

"That won't stop me," Faith said and punched Zaira in the face and chest and stood up.

She looked at Zaira, smiled an evil grin. Then Faith looked at the handle of the ice pick. The ice pick had broken off. Faith looked at her chest to see that she had already healed with the ice pick still inside her.

"Your right, sister; I haven't shown all the cards in my hands yet, sister," Zaira said in a dark demonic tone as she stepped back and seemed to disappear in her a dark cloud of flies.

Faith tried to track her movement, but it was impossible as the flies buzzed around. You couldn't see in front of you. She closed her eyes to try to hear Zaira's steps, but the buzzing noise messed up her concentration.

The only one that could see and move around without seeing was Zaira. She couldn't hear, so the buzzing sound didn't affect her. She felt vibrations of people moving in her body, and that is how she knew where everyone was. She went to Envy and punched her in the face twice.

"Ahhh! You little bitch!" Envy screamed, took off running, ran into a wall, and fell on her ass. Then scream as flies start to bite her once more.

Zaira's laughter could be heard over the buzzing sound as she ran and punched Michael in the balls and took off running.

"Ahhh!" Janice screamed, then shut her mouth as flies bit her and tried to enter her mouth.

Faith looked for Zaira but couldn't find her. Then Mike came from the basement with a can of hair spray in his hand and a lighter. He flicked the lighter in and pressed the button in the hair spray can, making it a blow torch, burning groups of flies. They drop to the ground, dead.

"Got you," Faith said as she spotted Zaira and ran to her and grabbed her by the neck, lifting her above the ground. Then, started punching her in the face repeatedly and refusing to let her go. Knowing she was too fast.

"Enough!" Black ice screamed in a demonic tone. His voice startled everyone in the house.

The flies flew up to the ceiling and hovered there.

Faith kept her hand wrapped around her neck. She looked toward her father to see he had Envy by the hair and his machete in his right hand.

"No, wait, what are you doing?" Michael said as his heart raced and pounded in his chest.

"Let her go! Father let her go now!" Michael said, gripping his dagger in his hand tighter.

"See, that's the look I like to see in you, boy. Be who you are. Your name is Evil; it's time you live up to it. All you do is fight your true nature. You're sisters embrace it. That's why they're so strong; they don't give a fuck. They find joy in the pain and suffering And know it. You do, too but front. I see what you can be. I see the darkness in you, Evil," Black ice said, calling him by his nickname.

"Shut up! And let my wife go now!" Michael said through clenched teeth as he tried to think of a way to get Envy out of his father's hands.

She can't die easily anymore, maybe if I rush him. I can get to my wife. No, I need Faith's help. I can't make the wrong move and lose my wife. Michael thought to himself. Then look at Faith, hoping she can come up with a plan.

"Wait, Father, don't let her go. I'll come with you instead." Faith stated.

"It's not you I want or need right now Bitch! You still have a lot to learn and need to get my grandbabies from that bitch and Lefty." Black ice said.

"If you know all of this, why didn't you help? Why won't you help me now? Lefty with the henchmen will outnumber me," Faith asked.

Black ice exhaled as if he was frustrated.

"No one will come to save you in life; no one is coming to help you in life. So you have to save yourself. Now save yourself. Let go of Zaira; she's coming with me." Black ice replied.

"No, I'm not letting her go, and I'll kill her if it comes to it. You'll help me and let go of Envy." Faith shouted.

Black ice busts out laughing.

"All of you act as if you're my only set of children. The original me would have been in his fifties by now.

I lost track of how many women I kidnapped and raped over the years. Over twenty-something of you came from my nuts running out here in the USA, three in Europe, and two in Africa. The list goes on. You four are only special because I see more of me in you than in them." Black ice said.

"Let Envy go now!" Michael said.

"I am bored of this," Black ice said, then looked at Zaira. He swung the machete.

"Nooooo!" Michael shouted as he ran toward him, but it was too late.

The machete cut through the meat of Envy's head and detached it right off. Then, the flies

28

start to make clouds and bite everyone in the house again.

Zaira hit Faith in the throat, got free of her grip, and disappeared in the black swarm of flies.

"No! Noo!" Michael continued to shout while crying and fanning as many flew out of the way.

Mike lit the lighter and sprayed the hair spray, killing the flies making it a path for Michael to go. The flies just left as fast as they came.

Faith ran to the open front door, and Black ice and Zaira were nowhere in sight. She couldn't feel their energy or aura at all. They were gone.

"Shit!" Faith said and punched the door in frustration.

Then, the sounds of Michael crying broke her heart. She felt it in her stomach. She turned around to see him on his knees, holding Envy's headless body.

Faith scanned around and didn't see her head on the floor and knew it only meant one thing. Black ice took her head with him.

"No! No! Why? Why! Not you. Baby, not you. I'm so sorry, I'm sorry." Michael cried uncontrollably while holding Envy's body and rocking back and forth.

"He took her from. He took her from me. Why? Why you didn't stop him! You say he's a father what kind of father does this. What kind of father wants me to hurt so bad.

God help me. Please lord. I did everything you told me. I pray every day, pray with my wife every day. Why would you allow him to take her from my son and me?

God no! What have I done? Why have you forsaken me, Lord? Please let this be a bad dream, God. Please, I can't bear this pain. But, no!" Michael cried hysterically with spit flying out his mouth.

Faith looked at him and knew he would never be the same again.

CHAPTER 3

Zaira held her kitten Danger in her arms, looked around, and knew she was in a compound in Chicago.

A big warehouse building that Black ice had constructed to look like a run-down building on the outside, but the inside was a different story. The basement was about the size of two city blocks. Henchmen dressed in all black walked around with a black masks on their faces. And some stood guard.

Zaira followed Black ice to his bedroom, which looked like a huge loft. He pulled Envy's head out of a bag. Her eyes were still open; he walked to a shelf where jars were full of body parts and heads—he stuffed Envy's head in a jar with a green liquid.

Zaira now knew where she got the addiction to stuff her victim's eyes and ears in jars. It was all clear.

Black ice placed Envy's head on the shelf.

"I've wanted this bitch dead for years." Black ice said as he smirked his evil grin, then turned around and faced Zaira.

"Do you feel sorry for her?" Black ice asks while talking with his hands in sign language.

"No, I was killing her anyway; I didn't care for her; I feel bad cause I attacked Faith. Faith looked out for me and loved me." Zaira signed back.

"Love will make you weak; your sister is very strong; I can make you just as strong. But you have to be willing to kill anyone, even your siblings if it comes down to it. Can you do that?" Black ice asked.

Zaira hesitated as she thought about Faith and Mike.

She knew deep down she never really wanted to harm them but could care less about Michael.

"Yes," Zaira said, lying.

"Hmmm," Black ice grunted.

"Follow me." He ordered and walked past her and out room. Zaira looked at him strangely but followed.

He led her upstairs to another part of the three-story warehouse. Black ice pulled out a cigarette with a crack mix, lit it up, and inhaled.

Zaira turned her head to look at him funny but didn't say anything; *the stories of being a crackhead were true. He still smokes.* Zaira thought to herself.

Where is he taking me? Is he going to try and kill me cause I'm not good enough? He keeps calling Faith his favorite, so what am I? Just another child he could care less about. I shouldn't have crossed Faith, but I need to learn more about him. She had her time with him. Zaira thought to herself as Black ice took her down a hallway and stopped.

He opened the door to a completely dark room and pushed Zaira into the room.

Zaira walked in and could feel the vibes of things moving and running around in the room. She turned around and looked at Black ice and twisted up her lips.

"Is this a joke?" She said as six hyenas ran toward her and were about to attack.

She turned around and looked at them as they stood inches away. They stopped and started crying, then sat down in front of her.

Zaira turned around.

"What was the point of that," she said in sign language.

"Pick one now!" Black ice said in a demanding tone.

"I don't like them," Zaira replied.

"You sound like a child." Black ice replied.

"I am a child or preteen." Zaira replied.

"You talk back too much even if you can't hear. Do you know the reason why we keep hyenas? We breed them." Black ice asked.

"Yes, Faith taught me. Hyenas can eat anything; Clothes, bones, flesh. The only thing they can't eat is metal.

If there is no body, there is no case. Nothing for police to look for; they can't call it murder or do an investigation. They'll just report a person missing and won't really look for them unless there's a kid, and even children, as long as they're black, they'll stop looking after a week." Zaira replied.

"Good, now, pick one and follow me," Black ice said

"But!" Zaira said; Black ice smacked her.

The blow was so hard that she spun around a dramatic circle, then stopped and held her cheek.

I forgot how much girls talkback over the boys. This is going to be long. Black ice thought to himself.

"I said pick one! Don't make me tell you again."

Zaira looked at him and wanted to fight. She knew she couldn't tell him head-on, but the fact he hit her bothered her. She had killed people for less.

"You can't beat me or out, smart me. You think I haven't been there and I don't know you. You'll be wrong now; pick one."

His voice was deep and low and sent chills through Zaira's body and the hyenas. It was as if something was speaking to you, not someone.

Zaira turns around, looks at the hyenas, and picks the one with stripes.

"Come here," she ordered it, and the hyena came to her; then she looked at one with a deformity; he was freaky, bigger than the others and had

two different colored eyes. One yellow and the other red, and his mouth was freaky big.

"You also come," Zaira ordered, and the hyena came.

"Let's go, three of you." Black ice ordered and led her and the hyenas down another hallway, another part of the warehouse. He opened the door.

"I want you to show me why I should make you my new favorite, or are you just another one of my children, and the only thing special about you is that you can control bugs."

Zaira stares at him and walks into the room, and the hyenas follows her.

"Can you kill everyone in here? The faster you do it, the better; no hesitations. That is what will get you killed, sympathy and empathy. That is your sister Faith's weakness: that and wanting friends," Black ice said.

"I thought I was going to learn something different. I thought you'll be different. Why are you smoking drugs? When you don't need to. You evolve as a killer and person; you stop holding on to the man you were and turn into something else. You're no longer the man you were; this is a new era, but you told me you started manufacturing drugs and fentanyl," Zaira said, then looked into the darkroom.

"So, you're putting me in a room to kill people, huh? This is childish. If you've been watching me, you'll know I killed my best friends, their mothers, and a serial killer, well, four serial killers. I loved my friends. Well, two of them.

Killing people has always come easy to me; I just wanted to learn why? Where did I get it from; Why do I hear voices in my head that tell me to do wrong? I wanted to learn how to fight better to be better than my sister. I'm just disappointed," Zaira said, then got grabbed by the neck faster than she could blink.

"You see, to think I give a fuck about your opinion. I will chop off your little fucking head and feed your body to my pets and stomp that damn kitten you always walk around with. Don't take my kindness for weakness, little girl, because you're of my blood. Remember who I am and who you fucking talking to! I'm not to be played with or taken likely. There is a lesson in everything I teach you or show you. Your sister listens to most of them. I want to see where your mind is." Black ice said in her face, then poked her on the forehead.

"You came from me, and I can take you out of this earth." Black ice said and grinned his evil smile as he pictured Zaira's head in a jar on his shelf.

"The daughter that talked back too much is the label I'll put on your jar. You children think you all are too special, but all of you are not." Black ice said, lying.

He had many kids around the United States, but only a few could sense when he was near, read energy in the air, or control animals, and Zaira was the first ever to be able to control and talk to insects. It's never been done. She had the potential to be a better killer than them all.

Zaira gasped for air then was thrown to the floor. She grabbed her neck and rubbed it while staring at him with hate in her eyes.

I pick you over my sister. You're a cold-hearted monster. Zaira thought to herself but knew better than to say something. She just studied him.

"You can stare all you want; you can't beat me. You won't even be able to come close to it until you can beat Faith. I thought you were something special, but you haven't shown me shit. Let me see your work." Black ice said as he stepped out of the room and shut the door.

Kitty's head was throbbing; she opened her eyes and looked around; it was dark and seemed to be a warehouse.

The last thing she remembered was walking home in New York from work, then someone grabbed her and put something over her mouth, and she lost consciousness.

"I'm too old for this shit. I'm forty-nine years old; who the fuck wants to kidnap my old ass. When their young women to get. Shit, my coochie, I haven't gotten wet in years; half you fuck face men don't even know how to turn me on. Just jump on top and start humping—no foreplay what do ever." Kitty said aloud as she wondered where she was and who had taken her.

She could hear women voices talking not too far away. She stumbled over some junk as she walked toward it. Finally, she hid behind a pile of junk.

"My knees sure aren't what they used to be, that is for sure." Kitty mumbled to herself as she looked and could see four women talking.

One was pregnant, looking as if she was ready to pop and give birth at any second, two of them looked to be her age, and one was a young girl in her twenties.

Kitty got up and walked over to them.

"Okay, which one of you kidnapped me and why?" Kitty asked, ready to fight.

The pregnant one looked at her. She was a dark-skinned complexion, in her thirties with a purples sweater on and black maternity pants on.

"My name is Jadore," the pregnant lady said.

"That right there is Shanay and Gabby and Laree and Bridget. The little girl hiding in the dark is Tanya," Jadore said, introducing everyone.

Kitty didn't even notice the little girl right away; she was no older than twelve, with brown skin complexion with two ponytails.

"Yeah! Yeah, I didn't ask to be part of this group meeting. I'm trying to figure out what is going on. What happening? Why am I'm here? Where is here?" Kitty said with an attitude.

She studied the other women and was sure she could take them; she was 5'11 tall and weighed three hundred pounds.

"Every last one of us just woke up in this place. We all were taken and kidnapped right off the streets. But, unlike all of you, I woke up early and knew who took me," Jadore said.

"You talk funny, where are you from? And who took us?" Kitty asked.

"I'm Haitian and from Florida; I was grabbed in Orlando." Jadore replied.

"How is that possible? I was just in the Bronx a few minutes ago." Kitty stated.

"I'm from Las Vegas," Bridget said.

"I'm from St. Louis," Laree replied

"I'm from Mississippi," Gabby stated.

"And Tanya here is from Chicago." Jadore stated.

"So how did we all end up here, and how do we get out. I do not understand this." Kitty said.

Jadore sat down as her feet started to hurt while breathing heavily.

"I swear this baby wants to break out of me, but now isn't the time. How we ended up here is simple. Most people don't believe it; you say his name, and it's as if it's a game or a joke—there are books about him, his the boogie man in real life.

Their stories haven't been told as much as they used to be when I was a kid, that when he was more sloppy, I was told. Now he cleans up even better. People go missing, and there is no trace of them. No bodies, you just never hear from them again," Jadore said.

"What are you talking about?" Bridget asked, but the other women already knew.

"Everyone knows the urban legend. But no one wanted to believe it was true or that it could happen by the look on all of your faces. You all *know already. He comes in a white or all-black van. It's the last thing you see before you disappear forever,"* Jadore said.

"But he hadn't been seen or heard from in years. Ten years ago in New York, it was a big thing that made five years in Detroit women going missing and sights of white vans doing it. Then it all just stopped as if it was just a story," Kitty said.

"What are all of you talking about?" Bridget asked.

Gabby looked at her.

"Have you never heard the story of Black ice?" Gabby asked.

"Yeah, it was a book or something; I read it once or one of them." Bridget replied.

"It was more than a book. Over thirty-five people went missing; no one saw anything, Just a black van driving around; we all knew who it was. It was him, the devil himself, Black ice." Gabby said.

46

"So, you all are trying to tell me a book character has kidnapped us and we will never be heard from again. This can't be true. All of you have lost your mind. I'm going to find a way out of here, which we all should be doing instead of talking about urban horror stories about the black boogie man. This must be a joke." Bridget said and laughed and looked at the other four women as if they were stupid.

"All of you don't believe this shit, right?" Bridget asked.

"You can believe what you want, girl. But that doesn't change the fact he has kidnaped us. Stuck in a warehouse, just like in the books you read, it doesn't change that the Devil is real and walks in human form as a man. The Devil's biggest trick was to convince us he wasn't real.

If God is real, we pray every day; you think the Devil is not real. You think we're all scared for no reason. But, if you are smart, you'll stick with us until we make a plan. Then, together maybe one or two of us can escape. I read newspapers when that happens. One of two women ran away from Black ice, but it took a group to do, and some lost all their friends so that it could happen," Jadore said.

"Psst!" Bridget sucks her teeth.

"We need real solutions," Bridget said and stormed off.

"So, what kind of plan are you all working on? If it's him, he will get us hooked on drugs and fuck some women," Kitty said

"Shit; I can use some good dick; if pussy was all he wanted, all he had to do was ask me. My man doesn't do the job; he has reached that age where he wants to sleep all the damn time. I'm thirty-nine; I only got finer with age." Laree stated.

"To be honest with you ladies. I don't think any of us will make it out of here alive. It's been years, close to ten years since a story was told about a woman being kidnapped. That means no one got away. I feel we are going to go through the same thing." Jadore said, rubbing her belly.

"How can you just give up and be okay with that way of thinking? We got to do something; you're pregnant. There has to be a way out of this place. I'm from New York. We just don't give up. I don't care what we are up against." Kitty replied.

"I like your fighting spirit." Jadore said while rubbing her big stomach.

Bridget found a rock on the floor and picked it up.

"Crazy ass old bitches, I'm too young to die, to give up. Talking about an imaginary black serial killer with pet hyenas. I don't know what this is, but this isn't that." Bridget said to herself, then she found some stairs and walked down them; she pushed open a door that led to another level of the warehouse.

This part was darker; she looked back.

Maybe I should go back. This shit is dark as hell; if I stay with them bitches we'll just be sitting around talking, not taking any action, that's not for me; they are forty and older, not knowing shit.

But I should have talked to one of them to come with me; Bridget thought then she could hear crying in the dark.

"See, this is the shit black people turn away from. So, why does it sound like a little girl crying? This doesn't seem right. I should take my black ass right back upstairs with them other bitches. At least I can use them as a shield and let them die first or get raped first, giving me time to think of something.

I've seen too many movies and read too many of Shameek Speight's books to know this isn't going to end well. Shit, look at me believing shit I read in urban books. I sound like them old bitches; there is no such thing as a boogie man or monsters.

This is real life. There are just crazy people. That's all." Bridget said aloud to herself, her voice echoing throughout the floor.

She slowly walked toward the crying and stopped when she saw a young girl crying and holding a kitten. Bridget twisted up her facial expression.

What the fuck! I mean, why this got to happen to me. I was coming home from work; now I have to be a hero and help someone. I want wine and my bed and a good show to watch. Bridget thought to herself.

"Hey little girl, it's going to be alright. Don't be scared. There are more of us that you can be with; don't be afraid. Come here, little girl." Bridget said, then took the girl by the hand

"Can you talk? You're very quiet." Bridget asked, and the girl shook her head no.

"Can you hear?" Bridget asks while bending down and looking at her. The girl shook her head no again.

"Well, don't be scared. There are no such things as monsters, just stupid men and people. We'll get out of here, I swear." Bridget said, then heard growling.

"Did you hear that?" She asks while looking around in the pitch-black area.

"Of course, you didn't hear, but it's something here with us." Bridget said and grabbed the girl's arm tighter, then started power walking at full speed.

The growling got louder as whatever it was got closer. Then a creepy laugh each through the dark, but it didn't sound human.

Oh, hell no! I'm not with the bullshit. This black woman is not about to die first in a horror movie or crazy shit. Bridget thought to herself, then looked and could see red eyes shining in the dark, then the laughter started once more.

"Come on! You are running too slow with your little legs, run girl." Bridget said as she tried to remember where the stairwell was at.

"Where the fuck is that staircase, I didn't walk too deep in here, but everything looks the same, and I keep turning around." Bridget said out

loud to herself, then she heard the laughter again.

"Hahaha hahaha." The creepy laughter now came from in front of them.

"Okay, see, no one's life matters more than mine. I'm going get out of here one way or another." Bridget said, then started running faster and saw the eyes moving faster and closer.

She looked down at the little girl and pushed her hard to the floor.

"You get eaten first. I'm sorry little bitch. It's you or me." Bridget said, then looked down at the girl sitting on the ground.

She expected the girl to be upset or crying. Instead, the girl looked straight at her as if she wanted to beat her ass. There was darkness and evil in her eyes.

"Why aren't you scared? Why are you not afraid? Read my fucking lips!" Bridget said while looking

confused, then realized she didn't hear the weird dog footsteps chasing her anymore.

"Ouch!" Bridget screams as she feels a small cut on her hand.

She looked at her hand, and the cut was thin and small, but the paper cuts hurt the worse. She looked back down, and the girl was gone.

"Oh, hell fucking no. See, this shit is not for me. I can't deal with this. It's too much for my heart." Bridget said, holding her chest and started wandering around in the dark.

Her body began to feel very warm, and her head started to feel light-headed, as if she was high. She stumbled a few times while walking, then walked straight into a wall and fell on the floor.

"What the heck is wrong with me. Why do I feel like I smoked five blunts and drank a bottle of tequila myself? My head is spinning." Bridget said out loud to herself, then she heard laughter again.

It sounded like it came from a little girl and the creature this time.

"To answer your question? I'm not scared because I'm what smart people fear." Zaria said.

Bridget got up and started walking, disorientated.

"What the hell did you do to me? Why do I feel like this? Why is the room spinning, and I'm so damn hot?" Bridget shouted but got no reply.

Her eyes opened up wide as she saw the stairway door but collapsed and fell sideways.

"What can't I move?" Bridget said and tried to get up but was only able to roll onto her back and felt like a turtle stuck.

She could hear footsteps getting closer. Bridget exhaled in relief when she saw it was just the little girl.

Zaira sat on Bridget's stomach and bounced on it four times as if she was a bouncing ball.

Bridget was a far cry from small. She had a nice-sized stomach and weighed only 180 pounds, but it made her fat since she was 5'4 tall. In addition, she was light-skinned in complexion, almost pink.

"What is this? What are you doing?" Bridget asked.

"You talk a lot. I'm deaf and know that. I cut you on your hand with one of my blades; my knives are dipped in different mushrooms, each with different effects. These ones were pretty fast. It will keep you still while I work. Did you know that most animals kill their prey in the jungle before eating them? Even the mighty lioness bites other animals on their throat, choking them or snapping their necks before eating. Well, I pretty much do the same thing with my prey. Only hyenas and wild African Prairie dogs eat their victims alive." Zaira said.

"Oh my God, you're going eat me. God, no! I hope you choke on me, you little bitch!" Bridget shouted.

"I don't eat people, but I heard someone in my family had done it. So I'm going take your tongue now. That usually is my sister Faith's thing. Mines are the eyes and ears, but you talk a lot, and as I said, I'm deaf, and you are still getting on my nerves." Zaira stated and took out a small leather pouch; she opened up on Bridget's chest; it was nicely packed with different size knives and other tools.

Zaira grabbed a razor-sharp blade and pried open Bridget's mouth.

Bridget tried to keep her mouth shut but couldn't. Whatever drug she was on made her feel weak and sleepy, as if all the energy in her body was now gone.

"I think I should vent to you; I usually don't talk a lot; I'm very self-conscious about it; I know I don't sound right off time cause I can't hear myself. The only person I really could talk to was my sister. But I crossed her and picked my father Black ice over her; I don't think she will forgive me; I regret

it." Zaira said as she started slicing away at Bridget's tongue until it was detached.

Bridget screamed, then stopped as she swallowed her blood and choked on it; she coughed and spat it up while crying.

She couldn't move but felt the pain deeper and knew it was because she was high. It makes her more sensitive.

"I usually don't cut out tongues that is my sister thing. She likes to cut out her victim's tongues, chop off their arms and legs, and leave them alive. I think that is too much fucking work to keep a person like a pet. I never owned a person before, but my father got places full of people he kidnapped and just kept. Maybe I need to learn." Zaira said, then pulled out a spoon from her pouch.

"Then I got an older brother. I don't like him; he thinks he's better than us, but he is just a killer, just like the rest of us, and chops people's heads

off. I don't think I can deal with having more siblings; it's draining.

Believe it or not, I wasn't always like this. I had a somewhat normal mother and another older sister, Crystal, But she got killed." Zaira said, talking as if Bridget was her best friend.

What's wrong with this crazy little girl? God, please let me move. I need to move my body. Bridget thought to herself.

The voice in her head sounded whiny and as if she was crying. Bridget looked on in horror as a spoon came toward her left eye.

"Ugh! Ughhhaas!" Bridget starts making funny grunt sounds while spitting her blood onto her face to keep herself from choking on it.

"Don't worry; I've gotten good at this. The secret to not popping the eyeballs is having the right size spoon and the right amount of force and pressure." Zaira said as she jammed the spoon into the corner of Bridget's eye.

"Uhaahhhh! Uhahhhh!" Bridget screamed the best she could and couldn't believe what was happening.

Stuff like this doesn't happen in real life; people get shot or robbed but never this, never a twelve-year-old girl sitting on them removing body parts and talking as if it was normal, just another day, or she was paying with a doll.

"Ughh!" Bridget screamed as she lost control of her bowels and urinated on herself, then farted and shitted on herself. Once her ass cheeks opened, she couldn't stop shitting. Even when she tried to clench her butt cheeks, she couldn't.

Tears streamed out her right eye as she continued to shit until she was lying in a pile of her feces, and it was on her back.

"Got it," Zaira said, pulled her eyeball out, and placed it in a rag.

"Stop, please, stop, don't do this!" Bridget cried, talking the best she could.

"I read your lips. You said monsters weren't real, but they are. My father is the stuff nightmare are made of. Shit, I was once kidnapped by a serial killer. There are people like my family and me out in the world. The world is not ready to confront it or see it. They hide it from you all, the police, and the government." Zaira said as she jammed the spoon in Bridget's right eye.

Bridget's body starts to tremble and shake.

"Stop that, stay still, or else you'll!" Zaira said and stopped talking as Bridget's eyeball popped.

"You fucked it up." Zaira said and scooped the popped eyeball out and tossed it into the dark with her tongue, then unwrapped the good eyeball and threw that into the darkness.

Bridget could hear something eating her eyes as she cried and could not see.

"I thought we were getting along well. I wanted to remember you. I was going to take your ears anyway.

You got lovely small ears, but I still wanted to put your eyes in a jar and look at them when I'm in deep thoughts. They always helped relax me, and I would have replayed this moment in my mind. I guess not now, huh." Zaira said and picked up one of her knives and sliced off Bridget's right ear, then her left, and stuffed them in her pocket.

"I would kill you fast as a courtesy cause you let me vent to you, and you seem very easy to talk to. Even though you pushed me to the ground and left me for dead, showing me you weren't shit, to begin with.

What kind of person pushes a little girl to the floor so she can die first so she can get away." Zaira said as she got up, covered her nose, and stepped back. She looked at her shoe and realized she had stepped in some of Bridget's shit.

"Ughh! Ughh!" Bridget made a funny sound as she tried to cry.

Her head was no longer spinning, and her stomach stopped bubbling. She tried to see, repeatedly, forgetting she had no eyes. Her world was completely dark. She heard grinding and sit-up.

I can move; I can move again. she thought to herself, then touched where her ears used to be and felt warm blood and a hole.

"This can't be real. This has to be a dream. This doesn't happen to people; this can't happen to people, not me; I'm not supposed to die like this. God help me." Bridget cried in her head then heard the growling again, she stood up and could listen to the growling right behind her, and she started running as fast as she could and ran straight into a concrete beam, knocking herself out.

CHAPTER 4

Kitty walked around and checked if she could find any windows, but there were none; she found a long hallway with twelves doors that led to small offices.

"How the fuck do I get out of this place. There has to be a way. I'm too old for this. I don't get this." Kitty said to herself, then found a nice-sized metal pipe on the floor, about the size of her forearm and walked out the hallway and back to the group.

"I found nothing but a few office rooms," Kitty said.

"I'm telling all of you there is nothing we can do; we can only pray that's it, but once people are kidnapped, nine times out of ten, they are never seen or heard from again, and I feel that's our situation right now," Jadore stated.

"I don't believe that dead ass we can find a way out. Whoever put us here had away out. Maybe we should have followed Bridget and see what is on the next level," Kitty said.

"I looked over there before Bridget even went; it's pitch black, not like here with these yellow lights on here and there. You won't be able to see your hand in front of you.

I'm not trying to be wandering around in the dark. That is crazy," Laree stated.

"That is the perfect place to hide the exit when you think about." Kitty replied.

"No, it is the perfect place for us to get killed and not see it coming." Gabby said in a thick Mississippi accent.

"Maybe we should just scream, and someone can help us." Tanya said she was no older than eleven or twelve.

"No sweetie, screaming in here is not going help. It's just going bring the people that put us in here." Jadore replied and rubbed her stomach.

All the women stopped talking when they smelt something funny.

"God, what is that?" Gabby asked.

"It smells like shit; I thought we agreed to shit on the other side of the warehouse in the dark corner." Jadore said.

"The smell was getting stronger." Laree stated while holding her nose then they could hear what sounded like someone grunting in pain.

"Look, it's Bridget. She came back," Gabby shouted.

"Why is she walking like that?" Laree asked.

Bridget had her arms stretched out in front of her and moving from side to side, walking in a straight path and looking as if she would fall at times.

Laree ran over to help but stopped short when she got close. She looks and lets out a quiet scream.

Bridget's eye lens was open, but her eyes were gone; it was just an empty block socket with blood leaking out. Her ears were gone, and blood was flowing out the corners of her mouth, mixed with saliva.

"What is it?" Kitty asked as she ran over to Laree with the pipe in her hand, ready for anything, so she thought.

"Oh my God! What in lords name? How did this happen to you? You were only gone for ten minutes or so," Kitty asked.

"Ughh! Ughh!" Bridget said it sounded like a newborn baby was trying to talk.

"What's wrong with her? Why can't she speak? We couldn't get her to shut up before." Laree said.

Bridget opened her mouth and showed that her tongue was now gone.

"Shit, this isn't right. This isn't right." Laree said and dropped to her knees.

"Dear heavenly father, please forgive me for my sins and help me get out of this place; I feel like I'm in the devil's house, Lord; help me escape this place. Heavenly father, don't let me end up wandering the earth with no ears, no tongue, and

eyes." Laree said, and Bridget started crying, but it sounded more like a dog when it's hit.

"Just great, you know all the right shit to say when someone is hurting," Kitty said, then kicked Laree while she was on the floor praying.

"Bitch you put your motherfucking feet on me, do it again. I swear I'm going bust your ass." Laree said and got up off the floor.

"Bitch, you're not going to do shit; if you were, you would have been popped off, so shut the fuck and stop fronting before I beat you down; there is no one to save your ass or pull me off you when I get started. So you need to relax so we can find out what happened to this woman so fast." Kitty said.

Laree looked at her and wanted to say something but thought about it and knew Kitty would fight her for real, and she was just all bark and no bite. Just talked tough.

Laree backed down and got quiet but not before she sucked her teeth and rolled her eyes.

This bitch keeps playing with me, and I'm going bust her mouth with this pipe and knock out all her yellow ass teeth. I don't have time for the games or bullshit. Weird ass bitch. Kitty thought to herself as she helped Bridget over to where the others women were standing. She helped Bridget sit down.

"What happened to her?" Gabby asked as she looked at Bridget's face in horror.

"I don't know, but it was fast. She wasn't gone for a long time, ten to fifteen minutes tops, and we didn't hear her scream, which means this building is soundproof." Kitty said as she thought about the situation.

"I don't want that to happen to me; that is worse than death. I'd rather die." Gabby shouted while panicking.

"Uhmm, Bridget can hear all of you. Shit, we see how bad her situation is.

If I didn't believe before, now I do. The stories, the rumors, and whispers of Black ice are true, but this is a little different.

From the stories, it says he collects body parts. Arms, legs, hands, even private parts but heads were his favorite. Bridget still got her head and her arms and legs." Kitty stated.

"Maybe he evolved and started changing up his killing, pattern," Laree said.

"Naw, I watch too much I.D. Channel and shit about serial killers. They don't change the trophies. They take. It's like they can't; it's part of them. Who they are. They can become better killers and better at hiding what they do, but they all still to the same routine—that is how they're easily identified. I don't think this was Black ice; I think this was someone else." Kitty stated.

"Why does any of that fucking matter? How is that going to help us get the fuck out of here?" Laree shouted.

"You're working my nerves with your attitude and mouth. I let that shit slide once; this is the second time. It won't be a third time; I dead ass promise you that, word to my mother." Kitty said in a deep New York accent.

"You New Yorkers swear you all are so tough." Laree mumble.

"What was that you said?" Kitty asked.

"I didn't say anything bitch but stop acting like you going pop off and do something; I'm a grown-ass..."

before Laree could finish her sentence, Kitty threw the pipe at her and hit her forehead.

"Ouch!" Laree screamed and bent over in pain

before she could stand up straight. Kitty was on her ass like white on rice, grabbing her by the hair and spinning in a circle real fast and letting go; Laree fell straight to the ground, and kitty was on top of her punching her in the face if she was a man.

"*Stop! Stop what are you all doing!*" Gabby shouted, and Tanya started crying.

"*You thought it was a game bitch, huh? I told you. If you open your mouth one more time talking shit, I will bust your ass. Now, look at you! Just look at you now,*" Kitty said as she punched her in the face, repeatedly busting her lip and her face started to swell.

"*Please stop! No more! No more, please. Get her off me.*" Laree cried, and Gabby stepped toward them.

Kitty turned around while still on top of Laree; "*you better not touch me, or I'll beat your ass next.*

This bitch is getting what she deserves; talking all that shit, blowing all that smoke. Her mouth cashed a check she couldn't handle. Mind your business while she gets this ass whopping." Kitty shouted with spit flying out her mouth.

Gabby raised her hands and backpedaled.

Kitty turned around and looked down at Laree, crying and covering her face.

"Oh, I'm going give your ass something to cry about." Kitty said, talking to her as if she was one of her children. She raised her hand high, and all the lights went out.

"What the hell!" Gabby said.

It was pitch black. No one could see their hand in front of their face. Then, a burst of weird laughter echoed throughout the warehouse floor.

"Ughh! Augh!" Bridget tried to scream and cry but couldn't do both. She could hear the laughter loud and clear and knew what came with it.

"Ughh! Ughhh!" Bridget made funny sounds while rocking back and forth while sitting in her feces.

"What is that?" Gabby asked.

The laughter stopped, and fast footsteps could be heard running around, stopping, then around them in a circle.

Kitty got up off Laree and felt around the ground until she touched her pipe handle and picked it back up.

"What the hell is that?" Gabby said.

"Shh, be quiet," Kitty said.

"If all the stories are true. I think they are hyenas. Black ice supposedly had hyenas in New York City, walking around as if they were just normal dogs," Jadore said, knowing this was the end.

"Shhh, I said, be quiet. I can't track it if you all keep talking," Kitty said, and her heart felt as if it would shit out her ass when she heard the laughter echo from behind her.

"Hahaha, hahaha!"

She turned around fast, bent low, and started swinging blindly but didn't hit anything. Then, finally, she stopped moving, and everything got quiet.

Gabby drops to her knee.

"God, please help me. Our father who art in heaven, hallow be thy name, thy kingdom come; thy will be done on earth as it is in heaven. Give us this day of our daily bread and forgive us of our debts as we forgive our debtors and don't lead us into temptation but deliver us from all evil. For yours is your kingdom, power, and glory in Jesus's name, we pray amen. Please, God, get us out of this unholy place, protect me from the evil one," Gabby said. Then she heard the laughter again and opened her eyes to see red eyes in front of her face.

"Ahhh!" She screamed, but the hyenas grabbed her by the shoulder and dragged her.

"Help! Help me! Please help me!" Gabby hollered at the top of her lungs. While kicking and screaming and punching the hyena but her blow did nothing.

She was 180 pounds and wondered how the hyena could easily pull her in the dark when even her own man couldn't lift her.

"Ahhhh!" She screamed loud once she realized she was being dragged down a flight of stairs and into the next level of the warehouse.

Gabby's screams soon faded. No one could hear them anymore, and the lights came back on.

CHAPTER 5

Kitty looked and could see a trail of blood leading to the staircase.

"Something took her," Kitty said.

"Why can't I hear her scream anymore? Is she dead? She's dead," Tanya said and started to cry.

"What the fuck was that. We got to get out of here. We need to get out of here now." Laree shouted and started walking back and forth.

"Maybe we should see if we can help her. She might still be alive." Jadore stated.

"That might be a bad idea if we all go down there together," Kitty said.

"Are all of you crazy? You all must have lost your mind. Something strong enough to pull a grown woman just came up here and took Gabby, ladies;

we're all on the heavy thick side; we're not small by a long shot. A grown-ass man can't lift me, and Gabby and I look to weigh the same. I got a little more gut granted. So we are going to wonder in the dark. That is the plan." Laree said, looking at Jadore and Kitty as if they had lost their minds or were stupid.

"I think we have weapons, rocks, sticks, pipes, whatever we can use. I got a feeling that we can find a way out down there." Kitty said.

"We are only going to find death down there; Jadore is pregnant, ready to pop, and Tanya is a little girl that keeps crying. All she's going do is be a little pork chop for whatever grabbed Grabby and Bridget here, have no eyes and tongue or earlobes, and smell like shit." Laree said.

"We're going to have to leave Bridget. We can't help her right now; after we get out of this hell hole, we can call the police and have them come back," Kitty said.

"Now you know that a lie, she'll be dead. I'm shocked she's still alive now and hasn't died from her pain or infection, but it will happen sooner or later," Laree said.

"What did I tell you about your mouth? That first ass whopping didn't teach you anything." Kitty replied.

"So, you're going beat me again for telling the truth. Lord, I feel sorry for the children you raised," Laree said, and then Kitty walked up to her and punched her in the mouth so hard that two of her front teeth flew onto the ground.

 "I said shut the hell up." Kitty shouted.

Laree held her mouth and looked at her teeth on the floor, then at Kitty.

Laree started coughing and felt as if something was stuck in her throat. She coughs harder and spits up blood and a tooth. Three of her teeth had been knocked out all at once.

"You bitch!" Laree said, talking with saliva and blood in her mouth.

"You are trying to get more teeth to knock out." Kitty said and raised her fist to hit her again. But stopped as the lights went out.

"Not again," Jadore said then they heard growling followed by laughter.

Whatever had its teeth sunk into, Gabby had let her go after it seemed she was dragged for miles. She quivered in the dark while touching her shoulder, scared to move. Finally, she sat up and couldn't see anything. Gabby flinched when she heard movement. Then the sound of a little girl giggling.

"What the hell going on? Please let me go! I want to go home! Please help me! I don't belong here. I got children that need me. I shouldn't be here. I'm in my late thirties.

What would you want with me? I'm no good to anyone but my children. I have high blood pressure. Shit, I haven't taken my medicine since I

81

got here. As I said, I'm not good to anyone but my babies. Let me out of here." Gabby said as she stood up and spun in a small slow circle.

"Ahhh!" She screamed as a knife was jammed into her thigh and swung down but missed the person who did it.

Gabby bent over in pain, holding her leg, and started limping away.

"Hmm, you should have fallen by now. So how are you able to still move?" Zaira said, knowing her knives were covered in mushrooms juices that had two side effects, one making her victim extremely high and two paralyzing them right away. But it didn't work on Gabby; she kept moving.

Zaira ran and stabbed her on the side of her stomach real fast twice as if she stole one thing from someone in jail.

"Ahhh!" Gabby hollered and kicked at Zaira but missed her.

Gabby started crying while holding her rib and limping away, hoping to find a way out.

She reached a wall and started feeling on it; she touched a handle and pulled it open; she sniffed the air and could tell it was a garbage shot. But, like the ones they had in project buildings she grew up in, the door to this one was much bigger that she could fit into it.

"Ahhhh!" Gabby screamed as teeth locked onto the fat on her calf muscle and pulled her to the ground, but she hit her chin and was dragged deeper into the dark.

"Ahhh! Let go! Let go!" She screamed while crying and could hear laughter.

She managed to twist her body around to see the eyes of the thing that was pulling her. It had one red eye and one yellow.

"God, this can't be real! Lord help me! Help me!" Gabby cried and tried to kick it and wished she hadn't. She kicks it straight in the face.

She couldn't see it; she knew it was a good blow. The hyena starts laughing. Gabby looked as her eyes adjusted, and she could see the silhouette of a little girl. The little girl walked past the hyena, pet it on the head, and then sat on Gabby's stomach.

"I can see good in the dark; I think it's genetic; whatever that means, we get it from our father." Zaira said all his children can, then snapped her fingers, and another hyena came running and stopped at Gabby's head; drool from his mouth dripped onto Gabby's forehead.

Gabby quivered in fear and started praying in her head.

"I'm Deaf; I got to be able to see your lips to understand you. You move around a lot, like a wiggly worm. I once picked the legs of a spider, and it still found a way to move around and tried to get away. You remind me of that spider. Now answer my questions. I promise I won't allow my new pet hyenas here to eat you.

To be honest, I'm trying to get used to them. I like my kitten, Danger, and insects better. But my father made a valid point. See, I'm from Detroit; they don't care about the bodies you leave around, as long it's not any upper classes white family, then that too close to home for them, F.B.I and police start thinking, what if that was me or my sister or brother house. Then a big investigation starts.

My father and my sisters kept trying to drill this in my head. If there are no bodies. There is no case.

Hyenas are naturally greedy. They'll get every part of you and still be hungry; I just realized why they didn't like them in the lion king. I'm off-topic. My question is, how are you able to stand and walk? You should be a druggie." Zaira asked

"Ahhhhh! Help! Help me! Someone, please."

"See, I thought we could have a conversation, but you're doing nothing but screaming. You know I can't hear you, right," Zaira said, then squeezed

her cheek with her little hand, then slid back onto her thighs until she sat on them and swung hard, stabbing her in the stomach pulling down.

"*Noooo! Noo!*" Gabby said and tried to move but felt weak out of nowhere.

Her body trembled uncontrollably, her leg shook, and her feet tapped against the floor as her stomach split open.

Zaira smiled, placed her little hands into Gabby's stomach, pulled out her large and small intestines, and laid them on her stomach.

"It's okay; you didn't have to answer my question. I figured it out. You're body weight, so it takes more time to affect you then you smoke weed. I can smell it on you. So your tolerance Is high. So for people like you. I got to drip my knives into something stronger. Maybe fentanyl; my father makes and sells that stuff now.

Crack isn't what it used to be unless you're in Boston or Maryland," Zaira said, talking to herself because Gabby couldn't focus on what she said.

She was in much pain to hear or speak.

Zaira stood up and wiped her hands on Gabby's jeans.

"You were no fun. The first one was more fun to play with. Let's see how the others are," Zaira said then looked at Gabby.

The word eat left Zaira's mouth, and the two hyenas rushed in faster than kids running to eat candy. One started ripping away the fat at her arms, while the other started to eat her intestines. That was nicely laid out on top of her stomach like a plate of spaghetti.

The hyena by her stomach starts to laugh.

"Hahaha hahaha," then bite into her intestines greedily and swallow chunks without chewing, while the other hyena ate the fat in her left arm.

Gabby cried and could feel her toes again. They were numb a second ago. Then, noticed she moved her arms and the rest of her body.

"Get off me!" She shouted, then hit the hyena on top of his head.

He ignored her as if she was a fly being annoying. He continues to eat the meat and fat off her arms as if she wasn't alive and cries for help.

"That's the thing about animals. They don't care if it's a baby or alive, crying for help. There is no empathy; They just eat. It's why I love animals more than people," Zaira said as she watched on in the dark.

"Ahhh!" Gabby screamed and managed to flip around onto her back and started crawling.

Her intestines hung out of her leaving a long trail and blood smear on the ground. The hyena continued to eat it while following her. The hyena with one red eye and one yellow eye got upset cause he couldn't enjoy the fat he was eating out of her arm now that she was moving. He started making chunking noise. Then ripped the meat off the back of her arm.

"You hear that!" Kitty asks as they walk down the stairs, each holding a pipe they had found.

"Yeah, but I still don't think it was good to leave Bridget upstairs alone," Jadore said

"What are we going to do with her fat ass? Use her as bait? That's about it and the only thing she's good for. You all hear that screaming just like I do; I honestly don't know why we're walking toward it, like the curious white people in horror movies. Black folks don't do that. We're breaking all the damn rules," Laree said.

"We're going because we all believe this might be the only way out of this shit hole; staying upstairs, all we are going to do is get picked off one by one," Kitty said.

"Great, now we will get picked off all at once, so we die happily together," Laree said sarcastically.

Kitty stops by the stairwell door, turns around, and looks back up at Laree.

"Do you want me to knock out the rest of your teeth? Now isn't the time." Kitty said.

Laree rolled her eyes, moved her tongue around her mouth, and felt the gaps where her three teeth once were. Gabby's screams got louder, causing them all to jump.

"I don't want to go," Tanya said with tears in her eyes

"I promise to keep you safe; I don't want to leave you upstairs, sweetie, just in case the thing that took Gabby might take you, sweetie, and I can't handle that; if you stay close, I promise my best to protect you, baby. Now come here's and stand right behind me," Kitty said.

Tanya walked more down the stairs and stood right behind Kitty.

"Hold on to the back of my shirt."

Kitty then opened the door and stepped in with Tanya right behind her then Jadore.

"Yeah, let them bitches go first so I can get away when it's time." Laree said, it took everyone time to adjust in the dark.

They still couldn't see but could see a little in front of them, enough to take a few steps at a time. Gabby's screams had stopped, but her whispering for help echoed through the warehouse floor. Kitty slowly inches toward her voice.

"Again why are we going toward the screaming woman? Well, she's not screaming anymore, but why are we going toward the scary noise, the person begging for help cause they can't help themselves? Again is that smart? I don't think so," Laree said.

"Shhhh! Stop talking; you going to let those hyenas find out. Just hush already, stupid loud bitch," Kitty said.

"*Help! Please help me,*" Gabby said while crawling still but not getting anyway. The hyenas are still eating her.

Kitty follows Gabby's cries.

Kitty stopped, and Jadore stood right next to her; they could hear Gabby as if she was right in front of them. They looked straight ahead and couldn't believe what they saw; Gabby was on her stomach, blood pouring out of her.

A large hyena had eaten all the fat off her left arm until it was bones. Now he was working on the right arm, pulling her skin off her arm as if it was skin from a piece of fried chicken, he greedily ate it up and licked his lips, then took a chunk out of her arm, eating a piece of meat and fat on her arm.

Behind her was a smaller hyena, eating the back of her thigh, with each bite, he would laugh like when a woman is dancing and laughing when she is happy when eating and getting good food.

"*Ahhh!*" Laree screamed at the top of her lungs.

A mistake she would soon regret. The two hyenas stop eating and look straight up at them, blood covering their mouths. They took off rushing.

"Fuck no!" Laree shouted and hit Kitty on her head as hard as possible. Kitty hit the ground like a ton of brick. She lost consciousness right away.

"Yeah, eat her! Eat that bitch!" Laree said and ran, leaving Jadore and Tanya standing next to the kitty's unconscious body.

Laree took off at top speed, trying to remember where the staircase door was. She looked back to her surprise; the hyenas ran right past Kitty; Jadore and Tanya were coming for her.

She didn't know predator preferred to chase their pry; rather than standing still unless they were starving, they'd kill the first thing they saw. But they love the thrill of the chase. So, like a cat playing with a mouse, Laree gave them exactly what they wanted.

Laree couldn't believe her luck as she found the staircase door in the dark, opened it up, and ran upstairs. She heard the door push open. Light in the staircase made it easy for her to see; she looked down and could see a hyena the size of a small horse with red eyes and a yellow eye.

He stares at Laree, making eye contact. His long tongue came out of his mouth, and he licked his lips and looked at Laree as if she was a meal from Popeyes.

Laree had never seen anything in her life more horrifying. Then the stairway door opened up even wider, and the second hyena walked in; this one was the size of a fox but had stripes on its fur. Again, he looks up at Laree; both hyenas continue to stare at her.

What to do? They're just standing there looking at me, waiting for me to turn around and run. But, instead, they're playing with me. This is some game to them. Well, I won't be your dinner and a movie. Laree thought to herself and started walking backward slowly.

With each step she took, the short hyenas started to laugh, but it would more like a sneaky smart chuckle.

"They're playing with me! Fuck you!" Laree said and took off running; she made it up the next flight of stairs and pushed open the door, and small it was more light on this floor. She looked back and could hear the footsteps of the hyenas approaching fast.

Think! Think! Laree thought to herself.

"Hello! Hello, you are all back. I'm in so much pain," Bridget said.

Laree smiled as a plan came into her head. She ran over to where Bridget was sitting at. There was a tube right behind and more junk and rocks.

"Hello, who is there?" Bridget asked and wanted to cry but could cause her eyes were gone.

Laree kicked her hard in the thigh so that she could scream. Bridget hollered in pain and rubbed her thigh.

Laree used the opportunity to crawl into the tube behind her.

"Yeah, they'll go straight for her. Get full off her and go back downstairs to finish eating kitty and Gabby. While I find a way out of the crazy zoo."

"Ahhhh!" Bridget screamed while keep rubbing her leg.

"Why would you do that? Why did you let me get hurt like this? God, why lord, just kill me. I can't take it anymore," Bridget said with her voice quivering. Sound as if she was crying with no tears shed.

Bridget started to tremble as she heard growling, followed by laughter and footsteps approaching her slowly.

"Do it! Just do it! Get it over with it already" Bridget shouted, ready to die.

She felt a long thick tongue lick her face while growling. She flinched, waiting for her death.

"Yes, get that bitch and leave me alone," Laree said aloud to herself while smiling, showing off the new gaps in her mouth from missing teeth. But she didn't hear any screaming or eating sounds like when she was downstairs eating Gabby.

"Something isn't right, or maybe they grabbed her and dragged her downstairs like they did Gabby's black ass," Laree said to herself as her curiosity got the best of her.

She stuck her head out of the tube she was in and listened closely and still didn't hear anything; she looked left and right for any glowing eyes.

"Hmm!" She said, then crawled out of the tube and stood up straight with a pipe in her hand. She sees Bridget still breathing and alive with no new wounds, just the same ones as before.

"What the fuck is going on here?" Laree said to herself and stepped closer to Bridget. Then her smell hit her nostrils.

Hmm, I almost forgot how bad this bitch smelled; I got used to the odor, but that explains It. Maybe they didn't eat her cause she stunk so bad, smelling like the shit she's sitting in. Laree thought to herself and smiled.

"You lead those things to me bitch!" Bridget could say, but it sounded funny because her tongue was chopped off.

"Oh, you can speak a little now, huh? It must have been hard to get that out; you sound worse than my three-year-old daughter trying to talk.

But yes! Damn, right, I led them your ugly ass. It would be best if you died than for me. All of you can die, but I'm going live and find my way out of here," Laree said, then Bridget started laughing.

"What so funny; go ahead, talk bitch."

"Do you think those things did this to me? Bridget was barely able to say and started laughing. She's here, and your following and they never left," Bridget said and smiled.

"They never left? Huh. Speak English, oh I forgot I you can't, Huh." Laree replied sarcastically.

Then she heard laughter then growling; she turned around to see the huge hyena with two different colored eyes, staring at her with his head looking as if he was ready to attack. Then Bridget's jumbled-up words played in her mind; she started putting them together like a wheel of fortune.

"They never left!" Were the words now playing on repeat in Laree's mind. The hyenas took off, running straight to her.

Laree stumbled and tripped on her feet; she hit the hard floor chin first as she panicked.

"Ahhh!" She grunted in pain, lifted herself, started crawling like a baby as fast as she could

around the tube, then crawled in halfway and stopped.

Inside the tube on the other end was the striped hyena. He looked at her and started to laugh his weird chuckle.

"Haha! Haha! Haha!" As if he knew they had outsmarted her.

"They can't be this smart," Laree said they couldn't as she tried to think of what to do next and tried not to cry but felt teeth lock onto the back of her right calf muscle.

"Ahhhh!" She hollered in pain as the razor-sharp teeth dug deeper inside her flesh.

"Ahhhh! Ahhh, lord, help me!" Laree screamed, then heard the laughter and chuckle of the hyena behind her. She looked at him as she was being dragged out of the tube. She grabbed the edge of the tube as she was pulled out of it and held on to it for her dear life. While the hyena in front of her like at her as if she was a joke.

"No! I can't die! I can't die like this, not like this lord."

"Oh, you won't bitch! Just wait," Bridget could barely say as she sat down and talked funny while laughing then smiling, knowing Laree's faith.

Laree's eyes opened wide when she felt a deep slice open up on the center of her back. She let go of the tube and was pulled out of it, and tried to reach and touch her back; it was like pain like no other. She wanted to touch her back but couldn't reach it. Then she tried to move her body, but it felt like her movement was getting slower and slower she turned onto her back.

"Why can't I move? What the hell is going on." Laree said out loud to herself.

"The fun part! The fun part is about to start!" Bridget barely was able to say as spit and blood flew out her mouth; without a tongue, words didn't sound like English.

Laree noticed the hyena that was biting on her leg had stopped. She lifted her head a little, the only part of her body she could still move but felt she couldn't hold it up for long. She couldn't see past her stomach but could see a little dark-skinned girl dressed in an all-black body armor-type suit. She pets the big hyena on the head. Then continued to walk to Laree and then sat on her stomach.

"What the fuck is this? Who are you?" Laree shouted as her neck muscles were too weak or numb. She lay back down.

"I'm the daughter of the Devil," Zaira said as she read Laree's lips.

"Get the hell off me and why I can't move." Laree asked.

"You'd be surprised how many times I get asked that. I have been watching you; you're a grimy ass bitch. You remind me of a friend I once had, Tatiana; Tatiana tried to kill me, well, pretty much did; I shouldn't be shocked, she killed her

aunt, who was like a mother that raised her and got pregnant by her aunt's boyfriend. So why would I think she would be different with me when she turned on the person who raised her and cared for her for years," Zaira said.

"What are you talking about? You're crazy!" Laree said.

"You're not that bright, are you? Tatiana Is smarter. I think it's time I kill her. I miss Detroit, anyway. But what I was trying to say is you're a grimy bitch; that's all and reminds me of another grimy bitch I know. So I'm saying I won't kill you. Not fast. I think I'm learning from my sister. It's better to keep certain people alive to suffer even more," Zaira said.

"Listen, you little bitch; when I get up, I'm going smack you into Sunday; get off me," Laree shouted.

"I told you I'm the Devil's daughter; now I'm going show you," Zaira said and squeezed Laree's cheeks, forcing her mouth open and

grabbing her tongue and slicing it away; two good cuts and the tongue was almost off.

"Ughhhh! Ahhhh!" Laree screamed and tried to close her mouth but couldn't.

Her body felt weak and sleepy. She had no control over it. She felt trapped inside her own body and was just forced to watch.

"Nooo! Stop! Stop, please! Stop!" Laree cried as her tongue was only hanging in by a thin piece of skin.

Zaira ripped it out, looked at her pet hyena, and threw it to him; he caught it in mid-air and ate it as if it were a doggy treat.

Blood flows into Laree's mouth; she continues to spit it out her mouth. Saliva and blood dripped from the side of her face and down her neck. Laree looked like she was dying with her eyes rolling in her head.

"Psst," Zaira sucks her teeth.

"All that drama and faking will not stop what's going to happen next. I did this too many times. The fake seizure act will not stop me from having fun," Zaira said, then grabbed Laree's right ear and started slicing her ear off, then placed it in a rag.

"Ahhhh! Why are you doing this? Why are you doing this? Please stop! Please, no more!" Laree cried out in pain, and Zaira read her lips and smiled.

Laree could hear Bridget laughing. As if she knew what was going on even though she couldn't see. Then Laree could hear the striped hyena laughing and chuckling; his laughter was sneaky and sent chills down her back as Zaira chopped off her left ear.

"Wait, stop this, please, no more. I can't take any more. I'll do anything, anything you want. Please don't hurt me anymore. I'm sorry for whatever I have done. God save me, please. Lord, forgive me for my sins. Please help me." Laree prayed out loud.

Zaira tilted her head, looked down at Laree, read her lips, and then pulled out her spoon. Laree looked at the evil, wicked smile on Zaira's face. She looked like a little girl, but she was far from that. She was something else, something much evil. Laree could tell she was getting pleasure out of hurting her.

"God, please stop this evil; Lord, you can do anything but fail me." Laree prayed.

"I find it so funny how most of you start praying when this is about to happen. I wonder why you think God would help you; I saw you hit one lady on the back of the head so you could get away. Then use the next lady up here as bait so you'll live.

Do you think God would help you out of all the people he could save and help?

Is he just going pick you, Huh? You out of millions of people. Why is that? Please let me know," Zaira said.

"God will save me; he will help me," Laree said.

"God is real." Laree screamed while crying.

"Yes, he is; I know because the Devil is real, and I'm his daughter. But God is not going to help you, no one will." Zaira said as she bent over and pushed the spoon in the corner of Laree's left eye and pushed it in deeper.

"Ahhhhh! Ahhhh!! Ahhh! God help me," Laree hollered in excruciating pain.

"God will not hear," Zaira said as she scooped Laree's eyeball out.

CHAPTER 6

Kitty rubs the back of her head.

"We need to go; you need to get up now!" Jadore said while holding Tanya's hand.

"What happened? I feel like I was hit with a train or a brick," Kitty said, rubbing her head.

"Laree, she hit you on the back of your head with a pipe and took off running," Tanya said.

"I think she was hoping the hyenas ate you first, then us, but the funny thing is they ran right past us and chased her."

"Ughhh!" The sound of Gabby moaning in pain caused them to stop talking.

All three of them cautiously walked over to her.

Gabby was lying flat on her stomach. All the meat and fat on her left bicep had been scraped to the bone, and on her right, it was just raw meat as the hyena just stared.

"Gabby!" Jadore said and bent down next to Gabby's face, and Kitty did the same.

"How can we help you?" Kitty asked

Gabby busts out in tears; "it's so much pain. Please kill me, kill me. I'm going die anyway; the little girl cut open my stomach; me laying on it and keeping pressure on it; Is the only reason all my insides haven't spilled out.

Please kill me before the hyenas come back or the little girl," Gabby said.

"What little girl?" Jadore asked.

"She's evil! The devil's daughter," Gabby said weakly.

"There's a way out. You just got to reach it before those things grab you," Gabby said, then fell asleep.

"Get up! Tell us! What the way out of here? Please get up," Kitty said and slapped Gabby on the face twice.

Gabby opened her eyes and started to cry, realizing it wasn't a dream.

"Please kill me; kill me. Let this be over. I can't take it anymore. I'm in so much pain, and it hurts when those things bite me; it's like no pain I ever felt before. They've eaten me alive and don't care. The more I cry, the more I scream; they just rip more parts of me as they like it." Gabby said, crying hysterically.

"I need you to get it together, Gabby; please hold your composure. Just a little longer and tell me the way out." Kitty said.

But Gabby starts rambling and talking in circles.

"The little girl should have killed me. Why she didn't just kill me." Gabby said repeatedly.

Kitty smacks her hard that it echoes through the warehouse floor.

"Where is the way out? Tell me."

Gabby starts to whisper. Kitty put her ear close to her mouth.

"If you find it in the dark, it's a wall before those things grab you. The garbage disposal is big enough to fit any one of us. It would take you out of here, but it's too late. The hyenas are back," Gabby said.

Kitty moved her head away from her lips and looked at Gabby strangely.

"What do you mean? I don't understand what you're saying," Kitty asked.

Gabby starts crying. Streams of tears came down her cheeks.

"He's back; He got my leg," Gabby said with her voice quivering.

Kitty looked up past Gabby's head to see yellow and red eyes glowing, staring back at her with Gabby's thick leg in it's mouth.

"Oh shit!" Kitty screamed and fell backward onto her ass.

Gabby hollered. *"Nooooo!"*

The hyena pulled her away, dragging her deeper into the dark warehouse until Kitty and Jadore could no longer see her.

"Run" Jadore said and took Tanya's hand.

Kitty got up and grabbed the pipe.

"Where are you going? I think I know the way out; slow down." Kitty shouted while following Jadore.

"This is wrong; we need to be looking for the wall," Kitty said as Jadore found the stairwell door right away, opened it, and dashed up the stairs holding her stomach with one hand and holding Tanya's hand in the next.

They ran up the stairs, happy to be back in the light.

"Wait? We just going leave Gabby and I think I know the way out we should go back," Kitty said.

Jadore stops breathing hard and rubbing her stomach at the same time.

"Are you crazy? You saw those things; you saw Gabby as I did? She's not going to make it; she's begging to be killed. I can't blame her; imagine the pain she's in. She was being eaten alive, able to feel every bite.

I'm not trying to go through that, and I'm not trying to wander around in the dark, in case you haven't figured it out; those things can see in the dark very well, unlike us, and you want us to keep wandering around until we find a way out. I don't think so. I'm overweight now, carrying this baby inside me and looking like the perfect walking snack to those hyenas. I'm going back upstairs where I can see." Jadore said.

"How long is upstairs safe? Remember, they dragged Gabby from upstairs, nowhere safe in this place. We can afford to get complacent and comfortable. We need to keep searching for a way out." Kitty replied

"I hear you, but I do not know; maybe after those things finish eating, Gabby, they'll be full, and we can try again. She is a big girl." Jadore stated and kept walking up the stairs and pushing open the door.

Kitty shook her head but followed.

"Everyone here is crazy, but for me. They rather sit than keep it moving so we won't die," Kitty said to herself.

As they entered the second level, they could hear loud screaming as if someone was dying. They recognized the voice right away and knew it was Laree. Then they could hear a weird chuckle of laughter echoing throughout the floor. The laughter stopped, but the screaming didn't.

Kitty and Jadore nervously walked toward it and saw Laree on her back with her hands by her side and a little dark skin girl no older than twelve sitting on her chest with a spoon bent over, doing something to Laree's face.

"Got it!" Zaria said, as she pulled Laree's final eyeball and held it up to the light in her hand as if it was a diamond, was checking its clarity. She took it and put it in a rag.

"I'm deaf, not stupid; you all just standing there. So, who is next?" Zaira said without even looking at them.

"Aghhh! Ahhh," Laree screamed in excruciating pain, making funny sounds with her mouth. Zaira got up and wiped her hands off Laree's face.

Kitty studied the situation; she looked at Zaira pull out a knife.

"What the fuck is this? You mean to tell me it's a child that mutilated Bridget and now Laree, you cut out their tongues and eyes?" Kitty asked in surprise.

"Don't forget I cut off their ears as well." Zaira replied, smiling ear to ear. After reading Kitty's lips.

"Girl, I'll beat your motherfucking ass." Kitty said and didn't hesitate to try to back up her word.

She charged straight at Zaira and swung the pipe at Zaira's head. Zaira rolled and got out of the way effortlessly. Then pop back up.

Kitty was enraged and swung again and again. Zaira backpedaled, then sidestepped. Dodging all her blows as if she was moving in slow motion, cause to her, she was.

"Stay the fuck still! I'll beat your little ass. You need an ass whopping and therapy. What the fuck is wrong with you. Who does this? Who gets happy off on hurting people!" Kitty shouted. While still trying to hit her.

Zaira rolled toward Kitty and popped Galway up, and stabbed her on the side of her stomach.

"Ahhhh! She stabbed me! She fucking stabbed me;" Kitty cried out while backpedaling, then dropped to her knees.

Zaira spun kicked her in the face. The blow was so brutal that Kitty fell sideways and slammed hard into the floor.

"You talk a lot, and too much. I could barely read your lips because you were moving them so fast. I want you to get up. I'm not done with you; I didn't even use one of my poison knives. Get up. I want to play with you longer before cutting your tongue out," Zaira said, but Kitty was out cold and had lost consciousness.

Zaira shook her shoulder a little and knew she wouldn't get up soon.

"I guess I got to wait; I'll come back to you in a few," Zaira said and smiled her evil grin while looking at Jadore and Tanya.

Jadore looked behind as she thought about running. But that idea quickly vanished when she saw the red eyes of the striped hyena behind her. He smiled then he started to chuckle, looking sneaky and greedy. Zaira approached Jadore fast. Ready to stab her.

"Wait! No, Zaira, don't do it; it was a test," Jadore said, making sure Zaira could ready her lips.

Zaira stopped in mid-swing just as she was about to plunge the knife into Jadore's chest.

"How do you know my name? What do you mean by a test?" Zaira asked, looking at her with confusion written all over her face.

"I was put in here to see how you'll do, to watch your movements. I carry your father's children— twins inside me." Jadore said.

"How do I know any of this is true?" Zaira asked.

"You're Zaira, and you're deaf. Your father wanted to see if you'll be soft like your sister." Jadore replied.

Kitty opened her eyes but didn't move. instead, she lay on the ground and held the wound in her stomach tightly while listening and acting as if she was still knocked out.

Jadore could tell Zaira didn't believe her; it was written in her facial expression.

"I'll show you," Jadore said, turned around, and walked toward the creepy laughing hyena.

119

"Eat!" Zaira said the hyena charged toward Jadore, then stopped at her feet, lowered his head, and started crying, making a whimpering noise.

"They won't touch me; they can feel Black ice children's presence. They fear them. Like they fear you." Jadore said, then bent down and petted the hyena, then turned around and smiled at Zaira.

"I guess you weren't lying," Zaira said.

Tanya couldn't believe her ears. She didn't know if to run or cry. Jadore was a part of this kidnapping and murder the whole time.

"There is just one problem!" Zaira said

"And what is that?" Jadore asked.

"I don't want any more siblings, overbearing like the ones I do have bitch," Zaira said and, in one swift move, swung her razor-sharp knife under Jadore stomach, splitting it open.

Liquid and blood poured out of Jadore's stomach. She grabbed her stomach and looked at her hands. But then her hands start to feel numb, along with the rest of her body. She dropped to her knees as she felt weak, then collapsed onto her side. She tried to move but couldn't, as Zaira grinned that evil smile of hers and bent down and started slicing where she cut open Jadore's stomach.

"Wait! Wait! What are you doing? Zaira stop! You'll kill them! You'll kill my babies!" Jadore screams at the top of her lungs while crying. She tried her hardest to move but couldn't.

Zaira looked at her.

"That is the point; after twelve years, I finally got my father to pay attention to me, and only me. I already live in my sister Faith's shadow. She's his favorite," Zaira said sarcastically and switched up her voice when she said favorite.

"He thinks she can barely do no wrong in his eyes. So there is my big brother; he just refuses to kill.

121

Because deep down, he loves him. So no, I don't need any more evil cute black ice babies running around here, fucking shit up for me. I need his undivided attention; I already crossed my sister for him, and I love her; she saved me and taught me how to think better and fight." Zaira said while Jadore screamed in agonizing pain.

Zaira pulled out the first baby; it was a girl. She cried aloud as Zaira laid her on the floor. Then she pulled out the second baby; it was another girl.

"Oh hell no, twin girls. Yeah, they'll be a problem and take up more love I'm supposed to get. It's survival of the fittest in life,"

"Don't do this, Zaira, please; your father wouldn't want this; they're your sisters. Please don't. They're my babies. Don't do this." Jadore begged and pleaded while crying hysterically.

Kitty sat up and couldn't believe what she was seeing, Zaira had done a full-blown c-section, and twin babies were on the floor crying.

Kitty looked at Tanya, covering her face with her hands while looking through them. With her back resting on a beam. Soon as Zaira raises her hand with the knife in it. Kitty grabbed her pipe off the floor and dashed to Tanya, grabbing her hand. Zaira looked at them briefly and paid them no mind as Kitty ran with Tanya down the stairs.

Zaira look at her hyena.

"Eat!" She mumbled.

The hyena chuckled as if she told a funny joke and took off running after Kitty and Tanya.

Zaira looked at Jadore, then back at the babies.

"My father's mistress should be smarter than playing around with the devil's daughter," Zaira said, then stabbed one of the twins.

The baby let out a weak cry and died instantly.

"Noooooo!" Jadore let out a cry that even Zaira could feel in her body and soul but knew she couldn't stop.

123

Zaira stabbed the next twin girl twice as the other baby. First, making sure they were both dead. Then, she kicked one of the babies into the beam.

"Nooo," Jadore cried and lost consciousness.

"Hurry, keep up!" Kitty said as she dashed down the starts and could hear laughter, footsteps, and heavy breathing behind them.

Kitty and Tanya made it to the next level and opened the door; Gabby was lying on the floor straight ahead and pointing to the left.

Kitty thought to herself as the door burst open behind them. Kitty looks back to see red eyes staring at her then the laughter.

"Go!" Kitty said and took off running, pulling Tanya, running blindly in the dark, unable to see, she tripped over something while running and looked down to notice it was bones of a dead person, all meat and skin picked off clean, she steps over it and touch a wall and felt

around and could feel the handle to the garbage shoot.

"She was telling the truth; I found it, Tanya; we will get the hell out of this place," Kitty said while opening it and looking down at it.

"Ahhhhh," Tanya screamed as she was yanked out of Kitty's hand.

"No!" Kitty shouted as Tanya was dragged away into the dark.

"Help me! Kitty, help me please!" Tanya screamed at the top of her lungs as she was pulled deeper into the dark warehouse. Then, the hyena let go of her leg and started running around her in a circle. But she couldn't see him. Kitty looked at the garbage shoot, then looked back into the dark.

"Kitty help me, please!" Tanya said while crying.

Shit, she's as good as dead; if I go, I'm as good as dead as well, and how would I find the garbage shoot again. I got lucky this time, it won't be a second time, but I got to help her. What kind of person would I be if I didn't try. Yeah, I'll be Laree's fucked up ass. I can't do that. Kitty thought to herself, then looked down and had an idea.

Tanya sat up, holding herself, trying not to cry. She felt the teeth mark leaking blood from her leg where the hyena had bitten her.

"Help me! Help kitty! Help!" Tanya shouted, then stopped as the hyena started to laugh, and it turned into a chuckle.

As he circled her. Tanya could heavy footsteps running straight toward her and knew it was the big one with the two different colored eyes, and her life was now over. She shut her eyes right and prepared to die. She was praying in her head, praying that it wouldn't hurt so much.

"God, please don't let me feel it. Please let it be fast—please, God." Tanya said in her head repeatedly, then flinched as she felt something warm grab her and realized it was hands.

"*Let's go now,*" Kitty said and yanked her up and started running.

"*You came back for me! Thank you.*" Tanya said while holding back her tears.

"*I told you I would,*" Kitty said as she looked down; she left a trail of bones for her to step on it to lead her back to the garbage Shot. She smiled cause her plan had worked. They made it back to the wall.

"*Ahhhhh!*" Tanya shouted as the striped hyena sunk his teeth into her forearm.

His razor-sharp teeth sunk deeper in her flesh and were now on her bone, and soon, he was crushing the bone in her forearm, going deep as he tried to yank Tanya out of Kitty's hand.

"*Not again!*" Kitty shouted as Tanya screamed in agonizing pain.

The hyena's teeth is strong enough to eat bones easily. Kitty swung with all her might hitting the hyena in the head. He bit down hard. Kitty hit him one more with the pipe even harder. The pain was too much for the hyena to bear. He ripped off Tanya's forearm and hand and took off running with it.

Tanya passed out from the pain.

"No, you don't die on me" Kitty said and picked her up and threw her down the garbage shoot, then leaped in herself.

She rode down the shoot, A stinky dirty tunnel, and fell into a dumper outside the warehouse. Kitty smiled. It was daytime, and she could hear cars and people moving about. She picked Tanya up out of the dumpers and walked down the alleyway.

She heard a thumping noise behind her. She turns around to see Zaira and the striped hyena at the end of the alleyway. Both of them are just staring at Kitty, not moving. As kitty walked onto the sidewalk and started screaming for help while running down the block. She looked back, but Zaira and the hyena didn't chase them as a woman jumped out of her car to help.

"What happened?" The lady asks while looking at Tanya's chewed-up arm.

"A dog attacked her. Take us to the hospital or call the ambulance, please," Kitty said and exhaled in relief as more people started to come to their aid, and some just recorded them on their phones.

"I'll make you pay for this one day bitch, you and your father, I swear." Kitty mumbled to herself.

CHAPTER 7

Tymack led the blunt while taking another shot of tequila. While looking out his condo view from New Jersey, he could see New York right over the water where he was from.

He turned around to look at Dutch tied to a chair with a staff in his mouth; he walked past him and looked at all the new cellphones they had scammed from phone companies that they would resale, then at the fentanyl drug on the table and blue crack.

Seven of Tymack's trusted soldiers were in the condo with him.

Three are sitting in the living room watching the basketball game, and two are in the back room with masks and bagging up fentanyl and blue crack.

Tymack was brown skin and African from Nigeria, and so were all his soldiers and everyone around him. He trusted no one but Nigerians.

Dutch was the only African-American, and he was a street worker. Dutch could see Tymack in his red versace robe, with his name, walking around as if he was Hugh Hefner as he smoked. He walked up to Dutch and pulled the sock out of his mouth.

"Oh, okay, nigga I gave you more than enough time to tell me what happened to my drugs and the rest of my phones and laptop.

We work hard to scam that shit. But, to be honest, I don't have any more time for your stories," Tymack said as he took another pull of his blunt.

Dutch knew he was dead; Tymack wouldn't believe the truth no matter what he said.

"I told you already, but you're not going to believe me," Dutch replied.

"So, you're saying a nigga came in. One man and it was ten of you all, and he killed everyone in the stash house and took my drugs, phones, and money, but you managed your getaway. But where the bodies at my G! because to me, it sounds like you're telling some American lies." Tymack said.

"I'm telling the truth; I know you all heard of Black ice, even in Africa and Nigeria, the man that walks with hyenas," Dutch replied.

"Man, that kid stories urban tales, even if he was real, they say he was a drug dealer like I'd. So why would he kill my men and take my drugs?" Tymack said in a deep African accent while smoking.

"I'm not saying him; he has a son; the son went missing for years, but in the streets, they called him Evil; that was his nickname because of the shit he did. Like his father, Black ice kidnapped people, mostly women, and killed men in his territory. But his son wanted to be some vigilante, fake hero. I say fake cause heroes are

132

not supposed to kill, but he went around killing people in the hood and collecting heads like his old man; he hit the stash house, only armed with machetes, and start killing everyone, stuffing heads in a trash bag, I swear.

He was cold and dark; He didn't say a word, just screaming and crying. A few of the men shot him, and he kept coming. Finally, he looked me dead and let me run out the front door, Tymack," Dutch said.

Tymack started laughing.

"You Americans believe anything and think we will be as stupid; that's why we put all of you on the streets to sell our shit. But you are feeding me bullshit right now. I don't like that shit; one man with no gun can't stop ten men; this isn't tv. People die when I squeeze the trigger—starting with you," Tymack said as he pulled a 9mm handgun out from his robe pocket and pressed it against Dutch forehead.

"I'm not lying; he's real, Black ice son is real, and something is wrong with him; he's mentally gone. Like he snapped somehow. His was dark, and he kept screaming," Dutch said, then stopped talking.

"Oh shit! I know why he let me go," Dutch said and urinated on himself.

Warm pee traveled down his leg onto the floor.

Tymack steps back.

"You nasty motherfucker. What's wrong with you? What do you mean, you don't know why he let you go."

Dutch looked Tymack in the eyes as his body trembled.

"He will take my head. He let me go to follow me here," Dutch said and started crying.

Tymack looked at him as if he had lost his mind.

"You're scared of him more than me putting a bullet in your head now," Tymack said. Dutch looked him in the eyes while crying.

"Yes," he said as the lights went out in the three-bedroom condo.

"He's here!" Dutch said, and his leg started to shake.

"Just relax. This happens all the time; every once in a while, the whole block loses power. It's even worse in spring.

There is no such thing as Black ice, Black ice children, or son. You just stolen my money and products; then thought you could feed me this bullshit story, like I'm stupid and was going believe, men walking with hyenas.

You think cause I was born in Nigeria, I'm stupid. I'm the number one scammer over here; I have a lot of money cause I'm smart. Not lazy.

I can get a hundred iPhones a day, tricking phone companies. Do you know how much that is *in one day? I resale each phone for $1300. So I make $130,000 a day, then I will be scamming unemployed and PPP loans; I'm up, kid.*

Us African boys have money, fool. You thought you could cheat us and walk away with our shit what you did with the Africans' bodies in the stash house." Tymack shouted in the dark.

"You're not listening to me; it's too late," Dutch said while crying.

Then the front door was kicked in; Tymack couldn't make out who it was; he could see the silhouette of a tall, muscular man in a leather pea coat, holding two machetes. One in each hand.

"Shoot that mother fucker!" Tymack shouted as Evil came in and ran into the living room and jammed his machete into the first man's chest, sitting on the end of the couch.

The guy in the middle raised his arm with the gun, and Evil swung down. The second guy hollered as his arm was chopping it entirely off.

He stood up in shock, holding his wound, and Evil swung, chopping his head off with one blow. His head flew in the air and landed at Tymack feet, spinning around in a circle like a bottle.

"You killed Larry; you chopped Larry's head off. Larry was my boy since my dapper days. You just killed Larry, you monster." Tymack shouted, aimed, and squeezed the trigger, sending five bullets toward Evil. Evil grabs the last guy off the couch, looking petrified and using him as a shield. The bullets slammed into his body.

Tymack stopped firing once he realized what was happening.

"Are you trying to kill me, huh? And kill my boys? Let go of ousman! What the fuck is wrong with you? What do you want? Do you want money? I got money," Tymack shouted as Evil held Ousman close to him.

He was still alive but groaning in pain and fighting hard not to collapse.

"Just stop this, just tell me what you want. We can work something out. I got mad money, dead ass millions. I'm one of the biggest scammers in New York. I can get you the funds. Just stop attacking my men," Tymack said, but Evil just stood there looking at him.

His vibe and energy was dark and traveled through the condo. His aura wasn't right. You could feel it in your body. Tymack knew something was mentally and spiritually wrong with the man in his home.

So Dutch wasn't lying, I don't know who or what this man is, but he doesn't feel even like a human. My body is telling me to run for my life. There is something dark about him.

"Listen, man, I asked what you want?" Tymack said again in a deep African accent.

"I want your heads," Evil said, his voice gave everyone in the room chills then he just screamed out of nowhere for no reason.

"Ahhhhhhh! Ahhhh! Envy!" He shouted while looking up at the ceiling, tears streamed out of his eyes, and he swung and chopped off. Ousman's head spins in the air for a second, and it hits the floor hard, sounding like a rock.

"No! I'll kill you! I'll kill you, motherfucker!" Tymack shouted while firing at Evil, sending a bullet at him.

Evil heard the back room open, and four men stepped out, two holding matchets and two holding Glocks with a switch button turned them into machine guns. They aimed, and hailstorms of bullets flew at Evil; he held Ousman's headless body up and used it as a shield, and ran straight towards them. Tymack reloads his gun.

"It's not going to work. We need to run. Regroup because he's going to keep coming," Dutch said saying while still tied down in the chair.

"I shot that ass hole; I know I did." Tymack replied.

"If we are still up here, we're dead. We need to leave while he's fighting the other men or he's going collect our heads. He can't be stopped like this. I had ten men with me. He ran through them as if they were nothing. The same thing he's doing now," Dutch said.

"Those are my boys, I'm not a pussy; you want me just to leave them." Tymack replied.

"Leave them or die with them. You decided because you're running out of time, and the choice would be made for you," Dutch said.

Tymack looks at him and unties him from the chair.

Screams echoed through the hallway where Evil and the four African gangsters were. Evil had grabbed one, pulled him toward him, and snapped his neck while looking into the eyes of the other three men. Two of them charged at Evil.

"I'm going chop you! I'm going chop you're ass up well!" One of them shouted.

Evil blocks his blow with his machete. Soon both men were attacking him, one trying to chop off his head, swinging high, and the other attacking low, trying to cut or slice his thighs in hopes of cutting one of the arteries in one of his legs. Evil block their blows with his machete, fighting them in the hallways that lead to the bedroom. The sound of metal crashing together could be heard.

"Die fucker! We are going to cut you good," The one with the Dewan said as he bent low and swung and looked up to see the machete came down on the center of his head, splitting it wide open and his face in face in half.

Evil yanked the machete out, and to his surprise and everyone else in the room, he stood up with his face split wide open. He wonders in a circle, then he collapsed to the floor, and his body started to flop around like a fish out of water.

Evil took advantage of the other two men, not paying attention to him but their dead friend. He ran up to the one with the gun and jammed his machete into his chest, piercing his heart and yanking it out as his body dropped slowly. Evil swung again, chopping his head off in one blow.

"You killed my boy! You killed my boys, you fucking pussy," The last one shouted while swinging his machete at Evil's face.

"Yeah, I'm going cut you up good then eat you like your some fufu. You're not so tough. Look at you; you look sad, like you want to cry. What got you crying like a little bitch." The man shouted, then looked at Evil's ring finger.

He had in a black wedding band.

"That is it! Your bitch left you because you're weak or have a tiny dick; that why American women love us, African boys. We got money and got a big dick. You don't have shit. Even your bitch left you," The man shouted.

"What's your name?" Evil said, speaking for the first time.

His heart skipped as he got scared for a second. When Evil spoke, you could hear and feel the pain and darkness in his voice. The man swallowed the excess saliva in his mouth.

Why did I think it was good idea to tease him like that? He did just kill six of my friends like it was an everyday thing. He looks crazy. Maybe I shouldn't have to point him like that; it agitated him. It's like pointing at a bear. The guy thought to himself.

"Look, man, I'm sorry; whatever I said, I was talking shit to keep myself from being scared. No hard feelings." The man replied.

"That is not what I asked you; I asked, what is your name?" Evil said.

The man looked at Evil nervously, his hand started to sweat as he held the machete tighter, looked down at his dead friend's body, and saw the handgun next.

"My name is Muhammed; why did you ask?" Muhammed replied.

"Because you're going be my first," Evil said and smiled an evil, devilish grin.

"Your first, what" Muhammed asked as he felt as if he was in the presence of a demon or the Devil himself.

"See Muhammed; my family has a thing; my father kidnapped people and can keep them alive for years while torturing them. No one ever sees or hears from that person again.

My little sister is much crazier. She likes to keep people as pets and calls it her zoo. First, she chops off their arms and legs. Then pulled out their tongues and made them deaf in one ear. Have them crawling around in all fours for as long as she can keep them alive.

Shit, my baby sister has a thing when she makes them deaf and takes their tongue and eyes and keeps them alive. You'll be my first. I'm going to keep you alive for years. No one will find you; no one is coming to save you. I will torture you every time I think of my dead wife, which is all the things me. I'll make sure you never die in my care, that this moment right here, you keep replaying in your mind, this the moment you might have gotten away or got killed fast. But you fucked up." Evil said.

Mohammed knew every word he said was true. He looked Evil in the eyes and could see tears escaping the corner of his eyes as if he was in emotional pain and had lost it mentally.

"Fuck no! Not me!" Mohammed shouted, then bent over and rushed for the handgun.

He grabbed it and aimed for his forehead to kill himself. Evil knocked the gun up just as Mohammed squeezed the trigger. The bullet missed Mohammed's head. Evil twisted his wrist, took the gun out of his hand, and opened his mouth.

"Wait! Wait, what are you doing?" Mohammed said as Evil grabbed his tongue, pulled out a small knife, and started slicing it off.

145

Mohammed swung, hitting him, but it was if a child was fighting an adult. Evil was tall and muscular. Mohammed was 150 pounds soaking wet. Slim built. He stood no chance in a fair fight with Evil.

He placed Mohammed's tongue in his pocket and punches him on the side of his head, knocking him out.

Tymack could not believe his eyes as he crept to the front door. He aimed at Evil, but Evil raised his coat to cover his face, and the bullets bounced off.

"What the fuck! Who are you?" Tymack shouted then Dutch pulled him. They ran into the building hallways and looked back.

An old white woman came out of her condo with a phone and started recording.

"I'm calling the police."

Tymack looked back to see Evil chasing them, looking like a football player in training with no gear running toward them at top speed. He pulled out his machete, then swung, cutting the nosy white woman's head off, then stopped. He pulled out a black heavy-duty trash bag and stuffed her head into it. Then he whistled, and four hyenas seemed to come out of nowhere, but they came from the emergency staircase.

Tymack looked back as the hyenas went into his condo and started eating the noisy neighbor. Tymack ran down the stairs with Dutch.

"Those are hyenas; he has hyenas," Tymack said, not believing the words coming out of his mouth.

"Yeah, he might have seen a few of them in Nigeria, But they weren't as big as the ones he was seeing now. Why are they so big?" Tymack asked *as he watched from the staircase door.*

"Man, you haven't been listening. All the stories are true about Black ice. They said he does something to his hyenas, that he's a genius and have scientist working for him, and they

genetically modified their pets. You ask why there are no bodies in the stash house. There are never bodies or police when these guys show up. They somehow jam the cellular phones, and there is no call for help. No video, no picture. You want to know the crazy part." Dutch said.

"What?" Tymack, asked.

"He is supposed to be the good son; he's supposed to be the one with the killing and only hunt his father and bad men," Dutch said.

"I don't think you got the memo about that." Tymack replied as he watched.

Evil leaves his condo with one bag full of money, another bag full of heads, and Muhammed's unconscious body resting over his shoulder, carrying him as if he was a towel, and his hyenas following behind him down the emergency stairs.

CHAPTER 8

Tymack rushed down the stairs and made it just in time to see Evil load the hyenas into the back of a van, along with the heads and money. Tymack hopped into his blue Mercedes-Benz.

"Come the fuck on before we lose him." Tymack shouted, making Dutch get in the car.

"Bro, are you crazy? We are going to follow him, is that correct," Dutch said.

"Yeah, and I'm going kill his ass," Tymack replied.

"Have you lost your mind?" Dutch asked as Tymack pulled off and followed the long black van.

"Yeah, I did. I'm going kill that pussy asshole. We Nigerians aren't like you, New York niggas. When someone kills your boy and people, you all do nothing; you just talk. I'll ride for him. Even make a rap song but don't do shit. If you think I'm not going to kill that nigga, you must get me up.

He just chopped the heads of people I grew up with and came to this country with" Tymack said and stopped as the van slowed down by a warehouse next to the water.

Tymack got out of the car with Dutch, and they followed Evil and the hyenas to the back of the warehouse to the sewer drainage they entered. Tymack wasted no time and started making phone calls and texting.

"What are you doing?" Dutch asked.

"I told you already, and I'm going kill that fucker; backup is coming, and we're going in

after him and saving Mohammed." Tymack replied.

"Listen, that's the most stupid shit I ever heard; we're going after a serial killer, call the police. We know where he's at. Call 911, and let's get as far as always from here as possible." Dutch replied.

"You sound like a pussy. Fuck the police; that man killed my friends; he will pay for that; how can we prove what he did? We have to get our hands on the heads he took.

There are no bodies. There was no crime scene; thank God he collected trophies; that is the only evidence we got. But I'm not leaving Mohammed's life in the hands of the police." Tymack said as Lamborghini trucks and Bentley trucks pulled up, Nigerians dressed in Prada from head to toe stepped out holding machine guns.

The group leader approached Tymack, handed him a gun, and hugged him.

"So what is the story? I knew you couldn't tell us everything over the phone." The leader of the group said.

He had on all blue and Cartier sunglasses.

"The guy who killed all our friends is there; he has hyenas and is very fast. We need to kill him, Z.B." Tymack said.

Z.B looked at Tymack.

"Hyenas? We're not in Africa anymore; we haven't been back in years. So what are you talking about? I bought twenty-five men with me. We didn't need that much for one man," Z.B replied as he looked at Dutch.

"Why the American?" Z.B asked.

He will come with us. Tymack replied.

"No, the fuck, I will not. Fool, sit back and think about it. He could have killed me the first time but let me escape, and I led him to you without me knowing. Now he allowed us to escape. He could have kept coming after us until he got us,

man. Instead, he stopped for no reason and picked up that old lady's head.

He led us here. Listen, it doesn't make logical sense; his father is a notorious serial killer that hasn't been caught in years. This guy has been around killing people since my mother was young and hasn't been caught. Do you think his son is going to be easy to catch? He knows we're here; he's expecting us. He is getting off on this some. That man is hurting. My mother said hurt people, hurt other people; that's exactly what he's doing," Dutch stated.

"If he is expecting us let's not keep him waiting," Tymack replied.

Tymack, looked at Dutch.

"You Americans are soft and lazy, and you're scared. You act as if this man is the boogie man or something," Z.B said as he laughed and put a toothpick in his mouth.

Dutch looked at Tymack because he just lived their experience with Michael, aka Evil.

"He's the fucking son of the boogie man; his nickname is Evil. Fuck right, I'm scared, if we go in after him, none of us is coming out alive, and Tymack, you know this.

Let's call the police, bro, and get the hell out of here while we still can, your boys don't understand what's going on, but you do." Dutch replied.

Tymack hit him in the head with the handle of his gun.

"I told you. We're not going anywhere; he doesn't even carry a gun. This ends now; he dies tonight.

I'm not calling any police to save my friend; I want revenge," Tymack shouted.

Dutch rubs his head and jumps in Tymack face, wanting to hit him.

"Go ahead try it!" Dutch could hear Z.B say from behind him while pointing a gun at his back.

"I'm not scared of you, Z.B, or you, Tymack. I have never been, but that man in there scared the living shit out of me.

You over here downplaying shit to your boys. That fool doesn't need a gun. We both emptied a magazine, and he still kept coming; if he did have a weapon, that was worse. This isn't street shit and street rules. This is something completely different. I'm out! If you want to chase the boogie man, you can just not with me.

I've seen horror movies; black people don't go into the dark ass hole, we don't chase monsters, we step away from shit like this," Dutch said

"Shut the fuck up. You heard Tymack; we're all going in," Z.B said and fanned the other twenty-four men to come on.

"At least give me a gun and a knife. I dropped mine at the condo," Dutch said.

Tymack looked at ZB and shook his head to say yes.

155

Z.B took a gun and a knife from one of his men and pushed them into Dutch's chest, and rolled his eyes.

Dutch looked at Z.B; *"I promise you, you'll be pissing on yourself in a few and wish you listened to me."* Dutch stated.

"Yeah, yeah pussy lazy New Yorker. Nothing new. Always have an excuse instead of getting money. You all need us to pave the way when you have been here longer than us," Z.B said and sucked his teeth.

They walked and reached the sewer tunnel. A double gate was the only way in and a chain a wrap around it with a lock.

"We need something to cut the lock!" Dutch said

Z.B shot the safety off.

"Shit bro! Why do you do that? So now he knows we are coming" Tymack stated.

"So?" Z.B said and fanned ten guys to go in ahead of him.

"Go in. Shoot everything moving and call out when it's clear. It's only one guy with dogs," Z.B said as ten men ran inside, armed with machine guns.

"He already knows you're coming, even if you didn't shoot off the lock. I told you this is a trap; next, they are not dogs but hyenas." Dutch replied.

"Yeah right! Hyenas in New York City or New Jersey," ZB said while laughing.

"You talk like you know everything, or you are smart because you know how to scam and take money from other people using their information. That is all you do all day.

Second, you don't know shit about New York. A guy had two tigers living in his project apartment years ago than another guy who had a 200 pounds alligator living in his bathtub, and you have a hard time believing there are hyenas in the city, you sound stupid. Sometimes you just need to use your head and shut your mouth up." Dutch replied.

"What did you say to me?" Z.B said and took off his sunglasses.

"I said you shouldn't wear sunglasses at night to do gangster shit stupid," Dutch said, ready to fight.

"Both you. Shut up and listen.," Tymack said.

"Listen to what? It's quiet," Z.B replied.

"That's what I'm saying. It's too quiet. I didn't even hear a gunshot go off." Tymack replied.

"That is a good thing. Maybe they got them. I'll text one of my boys now," Z.B said, then pulled out his phone and started texting.

"Don't bother; your phone won't work." Dutch said.

"What you're talking about?" Z.B replied.

"Yeah, he's right; it's not going to work," Tymack said.

"Why is that? Is he some secret agent? What up with you two? And you, Tymack, you have been around this one too much, you sounding paranoid," Z.B said.

"Naw, not that, but he has some cellular phone jammer." Tymack stated.

"The fact you were able to use your phone before and can't now, all you need to know is that this was a damn trap.

You dudes swear all of you are smart but don't watch horror movies. You just sent ten men in there, and we haven't heard a damn sound—that means run." Dutch said and looked at Tymack.

Z.B went to the sewer entrance and stepped in.

"Are you all good in there? You all got him." Z.B shouted but got no reply.

"We're going in; something is not right," Z.B said.

Dutch looked at Tymack; they both knew the men inside were dead.

He's just a man, yeah, I've seen what he did, but he could be killed like anyone else; we are supposed to be scared and walk away. No! He kidnapped Muhammed; I can't Dutch get into my head. Making me think this guy is the boogie man. He's one person. Everyone bleeds, and everyone dies. Shit, he was crying in my living room when Mohammed said something about his wife. Yeah, I'm going kill him. Tymack thought to himself as he forgot he was begging for his life not too long ago when he was face to face with Evil.

They enter the sewer drainage with ten men in front of them.

Dutch looked and wanted to run and knew Tymack or Z.B would shoot him in the back. So he was the last one to enter. As soon as he did, a metal gate came down, blocking the exit.

Dutch shook his head as Z.B and Tymack came back toward him and looked at the gate.

"What is this?" Z.B asked and wanted to blame Dutch.

"He's trapping us in, giving us no exit. Tymack and I ran and escaped, which was not going to happen again. This is where we all die." Dutch replied.

"Must you talk so negative, just manifest our victory?" Tymack replied.

"Man, all the manifesting in the world is not going to stop that evil mother fucker.

Come let get this over with. Stupid ass niggas. I told you all, let's run. I said call the police. No, all of you want to be thugs when I said this wasn't a street thing. Now, look at us. About to be killed in priced designer clothes," Dutch said while sucking his teeth and moving in front of ten other gangsters. Tymack and Z.B right by his side.

The tunnel was dark and looked like part of something else; there were little to barely any lights, making it hard to see. But a few of the gangsters had flashlights on the barrel of their guns. They walked deeper into the tunnels and stopped; there were three tunnels to choose from.

"How do we pick which one? I don't hear anything but steam pipes or see any blood or bullet shells," Z.B said.

"I guess we split up." Tymack replied.

"You got to be the dumbest; I think I'm the smartest motherfucker I ever met. You don't read horror books or watch horror movies. This man killed ten of my men in the stash house, then killed seven of Tymack, all before fucking dinner, without breaking a sweat, you all think splitting up is wise. All that we are doing makes it harder for us to get away and easier for him," Dutch replied.

"I'm tired of all this talking, one man who got the drop on you and Tymack. I'll put a bullet between his head and call it a night.

Tymack, I don't know what's up with you, bro; stop letting the American get in your head; let's finish this and get back to this money; I got more scams to do," Z.B said and moved close to Tymack so only he could hear him.

"And after we kill this Evil guy, we would take care of Dutch we can't trust any American. He might snitch later on—a chance I'm unwilling to take. You feel me," Z.B said.

"Yeah, I'm with that; I don't know how I let him get in my head. Let's finish this." Tymack replied.

"You three with us, and the rest of you split off in two groups of three and go down the other tunnels; if you see anything, scream; if you find the other men, let me know. If you hear gunshots run toward them. This guy is fast, and this is his spot, so stay on point.

The nigga looks like a muscle candy man. If you see anyone looking like that, kill him and fast." Tymack said.

Then he pushed Dutch.

"You lead fool."

Dutch looked back at him. "Really! Let me die first; the only one that manages to live twice after encountering this psychopath, shit, I might be our only way out of this place," Dutch said, looking at Tymack.

Tymack looked at Z.B and didn't want to seem soft but knew Dutch was right.

"Just keep going," Tymack ordered.

Dutch shook his head and entered the tunnel; he scanned the tunnel looking for ways out if he had to run. He knew going back wasn't the answer. He looked up, and there was nothing but pipes.

Air got to be coming in here somehow; if I can find the vents, that could be my way out because I can feel the fresh breeze, it doesn't stink down here like it is supposed to; it's a sewer, right, or is it. It looks like it's part of that warehouse and something underneath it—Dutch thought to himself.

"I think we are under the warehouse," Dutch said to Tymack.

"Shut the fuck up and keep walking, fool," Z.B said.

"Again that's why I said all of you are stupid motherfuckers dipped in designer clothes; I'm trying to figure a way out of here for us when shit hits the fan, and shit will hit the fan," Dutch said, and Z.B hit him on the back of the head with the handle of his gun.

Dutch stumbled forward and rubbed his head, and turned around in anger.

"Go ahead; I dare you, Yankee boy," Z.B said.

"When he comes for us, I will make sure you don't escape. You fuck face." Dutch shouted with spit flying out his mouth.

"Pussy ass, waiting for some nigga you are scared of to finish me instead of trying to do it yourself. All men bleed, and I'll show you that," Z.B said.

"You two shut the fuck up. Do you hear that?" Tymack said.

Everyone got quiet. The sound of men groaning in pain and crying could be heard coming from the end of the tunnel.

"Man, we need to turn around. I got a bad feeling; we're about to get killed by baby Black ice," Dutch said.

"Those are stories, that is it, tales of an American coming to Africa to buy hyenas, and bringing them back to the states. There is no such thing as a black serial killer. He would be locked up or dead already; the police kill black men for fun and get away with it. What makes him so special, huh?" Z.B said

166

"I have a homie who believes in conspiracies and said they couldn't stop Black ice, so the government made a deal with him; he can kill who he wants, as long it wasn't the rich and elite, its population control anyway. But this is his son, and something wrong with him; you didn't see him, Tymack did. Something snapped in his mind; he wasn't all there." Dutch replied.

"There is no such thing as Black ice; now come in and shut up."

"You're going pray that you were wrong and listened to me," Dutch said as his stomach bubbled up with fear.

The sound grew louder as they came to the end of the tunnel that exited and turned left real fast and pointed their guns to see the other group of men.

All three tunnels lead to the same one run. They all looked at each other, relaxed, and lowered their guns. The room was pitched black. A loud rumbling sound could be heard as gates came down behind them, sealing off the three tunnels to get out.

Dutch ran to it and tried to lift the gate but couldn't. He turned around and kept his back against the gate, holding his gun tightly.

Tymack backpedaled and stood next to him, knowing Dutch had an act of escaping bad situations. Then, the flashlight on all the guns stops working.

"What the hell going on?" Z.B said, banging on the flashlight in his machine gun.

"It's an emp, an electric pulse wave. It kills all electric devices—" Dutch mumble.

"They don't have that type of stuff in the hood," Z.B said and stood next to him.

"I told all of you this isn't any good shit; this is something else. Something worse. This is the Devil, and we're in his playground," Dutch said just as lights start flashing off and on really fast

like stroke lights, it hurt to keep your eyes open, but in a brief second, you could see.

All the men screamed the second time the light came on; the first ten men that entered their bodies were torn to shreds, body parts everywhere, and large hyenas, more than twenty, was bent over, eating them. A man held two machetes in its center, one in each hand with a king pea coat on and no shirt. He smiled an evil grin then the lights went out.

"Ahhh!" The man on the left tunnel hollered as he opened up fire, sending a hail of bullets in every direction, but a hyena grabbed him by the legs, pulled him away from his friend, sunk his teeth into his stomach, and started eating.

His screams of pain echoed through the room didn't last as another hyena opened his mouth, and his jaw stretched wide, and he ate the top half of the man's skull, hair and brain dripping out his mouth as he took another bite of the man face.

The African gangsters started to panic; while firing, one shot his friend, thinking he was a hyena. He backpedaled and could hear laughter behind him. He tried to turn and fire but wasn't fast enough as two hyenas leaped on top of him, knocking him to the ground and dragged him into the dark.

"What is this? What the fuck going on?" Z.B shouted while shooting in the dark.

The lights came on and off a few more times fast. Dutch scan the room and could see a door across the room, past all the dead bodies and hyenas.

That is the room he came out of, is the way out, or at least out of here. Dutch thought to himself as he tried to remember every detail of the large room; one of the African gangsters saw a hyena's red eyes running straight toward him.

He fired, sending a spray of bullets into its face and chest, and smiled as the hyena slid across the floor and lay dead in front of his feet.

"I got one!" He shouted and was his last words as Evil swung and chopped off his head, then picked it up and stuffed it into a bag. He dropped the bag, ran up to another African gangster, stabbed him in the chest, and knocked the gun out of his hand.

"Ahhh!" The man screamed as Evil pushed him toward a hyena, then grabbed the man and dragged him away.

"We need to go!" Dutch said over the screaming and crying.

"Go where" Tymack said.

"We have to run past the hyenas. It's the only way out of this room. If we are still here, we're going to die," Dutch said.

"Fuck that! I say we shoot that nigga and the hyenas," Z.B replied.

"Incase you haven't been paying attention, that is not working, and it's only a matter of time before all your men are dead, and the focus will

be on us. Tymack this how we escape before. We got to run together. It's the only way, and we got to do it now." Dutch said.

"You ran while your friends were being killed, Tymack; you let this American influence you," Z.B said, not believing his ears.

But flashing of an orange light came out the gun's muzzle to the men on the far right of him; the lights lit up the dark for a brief second since the white light stopped flashing, Z.B could see three hyenas play toggle war with one of his men. One had his leg, and the other two had his arms; they pulled until his limbs ripped off and started eating it.

Z.B could see Evil bent over, chopping up one of his men.

Z.B aimed and fired, sending multiple bullets slamming into his back. They bounced off his bulletproof leather pea coat.

Evil stood up straight, then turned around, looking at Z.B in slow motion.

"You'll be my second," Evil said and started to run in his direction.

"Oh shit! Okay, let's go, let's go," Z.B said and started running.

"No, this way," Dutch said as he ran in front of him.

He knew it was an opening pathway, straight through the hyenas feeding grounds, and they all wouldn't make it.

"Shit, I pray one of them gets eaten, not me, Lord. Please let me live through this. I promise not to scam anymore, or PPP loans, or sell drugs. Just let me get the hell out of here. It would be my third time asking for a miracle tonight, but my God can do anything but fail. Lord Jesus, I know you're real because I'm in the house of the devil himself. Protect me and let me get home to my children." Dutch prayed in his head as he ran.

Screams from men dying echoed throughout the room, along with gunfire and laughter from hyenas. Soon the gunfire had slowed down, and only screams of men being ripped apart could be heard.

"This way," Dutch said as he tried to remember the pathway, Tymack right behind him, two more African gangsters in the middle, and Z.B last. He could see Evil running toward him.

"Ahhh!" One of the African gangsters screamed as a hyena locked his teeth into his shoulder and took him into the dark, next to the others.

His friend stopped and fired in their direction. Z.B wasted no time running past him, knowing Evil was on his ass like white on rice.

"Who is this guy?" Z.B said as he turned around and fired three shots at Evil.

Evil raises his coat and covers his face with it, and the bullet bends off. Z.B turned back around continues running.

"Getaway, boss, go," the man Z.B passed shouted as he wrapped his arms around Evil in hopes to slow him down or hold him still.

Dutch could barely see but tried to remember to stay straight. The laughter of the hyenas got louder as they ripped the flesh off the bodies of the dead men, some men could be heard crying and trying to fight the hyenas. Dutch tried to block all the sounds out.

"Please don't let one of those things jump out and grab me, Lord. Please, I want to live; remember God, I didn't even want to come here. I knew what it was from the jump; I promised to stop eating meat and pray every day. So please just let me make it out here. Bless me one more time; I promise I won't be a gangster anymore." Dutch prayed as he got tired but kept running.

I should have listened to Dutch ass; now look at me, running from this big, scary motherfucker again. Who keeps hyenas in the city, and why are they so big. I'm going back to Nigeria and staying there for a while. This is just too much for me. Tymack thought to himself.

"We made it," Dutch said as he reached the streak door, he pushed it open.

Z.B looked back to see Evil flip his friend that was holding him. Over his shoulder, then chop off both his arms.

"Ahhhhh!" The African gangster's scream was cut short as Evil chopped off his head, picked it up, walked to his garbage bag, and placed it in.

Dutch pushed the door open some more it made a creaking sound, then everything got quiet. The room was silent.

Dutch, Tymack, and Z.B turned around to see red glowing eyes from all the hyenas staring at them and Evil standing in the middle of them, looking at Dutch, Tymack, and Z.B.

"This shit is crazy; I'm not dying here, not like this," Tymack said and ran past Dutch, and Z.B did the same.

Dutch looked at Evil.

"Mr. Evil or Michael, I have nothing to do with this shit, sir!" Dutch said, and Evil took off, running toward him at top speed.

"Fuck! Fuck!" Dutch said as he went through the door and realized he could not lock it.

"Help me shut it." Dutch said.

Z.B, and Tymack, just looked at his struggle to push the door shut.

Dutch manged to close it and closed the lock bolt, just as Evil ran into the door with his body weight.

"Thanks for the damn help," Dutch said sarcastically and stepped back from the steel door.

The door shook every time Evil threw his body into it.

"I don't think it will hold," Dutch said.

"It's a steel door; he's not getting through that." Z.B replied, then saw the door frame shake when Evil ran into the door again.

"Yeah, I think you're right." Z.B replied.

"Come on. Let's keep it moving before he gets in here. We got to find a way," Dutch said.

"How are we going to find a way out? We're underground." Z.B replied.

"Yeah, but as I said, I think we're underneath that warehouse we park next to; all we got to do is find a way up. Make it to a car, get out of here, and don't look back." Dutch replied.

"This has to be hell; I emptied my gun at him. He just kept coming. I can't get the screams of my friends out of my head," Z.B said, holding back his tears.

"I try to warn you about this; Tymack knew but insisted that we did this. Now, look at us," Dutch said.

Tymack pointed his gun at Dutch head.

"Kill me! Go ahead; it's better than getting eaten by hyenas or having that man chop off my head; you both have no chance of getting out of here without me, so lower the gun and stop wasting *time,*" Dutch said as the loud thump from the door slammed caused them to flinch.

"*Let's go,*" Dutch said and started walking while looking up at the vents.

There were light in the tunnels, not much just a lightbulb every few feet on the side of the walls. A cold breeze could be felt.

"*Why is it so cold back here?*" Z.B asked as he runs his palms through his skin.

"*I'm afraid to find out.*" Dutch replied as he tried not to think the worse.

There was only one door in front of them. Dutch pushes it open, and cold air rush in his face as he steps in.

A blue light was on in the large room. Tymack and Z.B followed closely behind Dutch.

"*What is this place?*"

"*I think this is where he sleeps,*" Dutch said as he noticed a bed and couch on the far side of the room. But that was not what had his attention. Sitting next to the bed was a thick brown-skinned woman's body with no head.

Dutch walked over to it and studied the body. She was dressed in designer cloth, and she was well taken care of, then he noticed the wedding ring in her hand.

"You guys, I think this is his wife," Dutch said.

"Shit, he's sick, so he chopped her head off and fucks her body now; that's why it's so cold in here, to keep her from rotting." Tymack stated.

"Naw, I think it's more to it, the story goes. Michael was good but killed once in a while; this is the guy that ran across us; he isn't that person anymore. Remember he killed the old white lady in your condo. How is he a good guy if he did that? I think something happened to his wife, and he snapped. The dude went completely dark and lost his mind." Dutch replied.

"That doesn't explain a lot. So, why start killing, and what's with the hyenas?" Z.B asked.

"Have you not been paying attention? If your father is a notorious serial killer, that's what you grow up seeing and knowing; that shit is in you.

The stuff we're freaking out about right now is his Sunday, fucking normal. He's desensitized to all of this shit, taking heads and killing.

This is just another Monday for him right now; to us, it's like, what the fuck?" Dutch replied.

"I don't care what anyone says; this shit is not usual; it's straight out of a horror movie; this is some sick shit; I've never been so scared." Z.B replied

"You are scared now; wait till you see what he does with the heads." Dutch said as he opened the door and entered another room. Tymack followed; this room was colder than the last one. A green light hung from the tall ceiling. There were shelves on both sides of the room with big jars and people's heads.

Tymack eyes opened wide as he saw a few of his friends, his next-door neighbor, the old shire woman's head floating in a thick liquid. All their eyes were open as if they were looking at them; there were more empty jars as they walked down the room.

"This is some sick shit, this some twisted shit here." Z.B said as he started to panic.

"I told you from the jump this wasn't any street drama; this was something else.

We should have called the police right away. If we got out of this place, I'm calling the cops; I don't care about that snitch shit. The damn F.B.I need to come and stop this man; I counted over twenty heads in jars and over forty empty jars. He is not a man, but a damn monster," Z.B said they got quiet when they heard a man crying.

They walked to the end of the room and saw another door. Dutch pushed it open.

The room was dark, and the ceiling was tall; Dutch looked up and could see the vent, then a ladder that led to a door on the ceiling.

"Look up there? I think that our way out of here, I bet that door on the ceiling leads to the warehouse, and from there, we can get to the cars and never look back," Dutch said.

"Tymack look at Z.B and grinned, then they heard the sound of the man groaning in pain.

"What is that?" Z.B said.

"I know that voice; Muhammed, is that you? I come to save you, my friend. Don't worry; I'll get you out of here." Tymack said and ran to the far side of the room.

The room had a yellow light bulb on the wall, but there wasn't another. The room was too big, and the spot was still dark.

"Look the Ladder," Dutch said, then started thinking.

This seems too easy; why would the ladder to the warehouse be on the wall while he got Muhammed in here. It's not adding up, something wrong. Dutch thought to himself.

183

"Ahhh!" Tymack screamed as he reached the wall, Muhammed was chained to the wall by his hands.

"Why are you screaming like a girl?" Z.B asked and walked over, his eyes opened up wide.

Muhammed's ears had been cut off and his tongue cut out. But that wasn't the worse part. All the skin on his face had been peeled off, and starting from his left hand down to his chest, the skin is peeled off but hung on him like a shirt, as if the person wasn't done, the right half of his chest and arms still had the skin on it.

"What kind of animal is he. Why would he do this to a person?" Tymack said as his body trembled in fear.

"Ughhhh!" Muhammed managed to say.

"Kill me! Kill me!" He tried to say, but it was hard to make out the words since he didn't have a tongue. Just drool and blood leaked out of his mouth.

"What is he trying to say?" Dutch asked.

"He said kill him, but what would be the fun in that. I'm not done with him yet."

Tymack, Dutch, and Z.B heard the voice say from behind them.

Z.B passed gas and shitted on himself just a little. Then, all three men turn around to see Evil standing in the middle of the room.

"He's my first; I'm going keep him alive for years after finishing peeling his skin off, you'll be my second and third and fourth, hearing your hopeless cries will do something to me and ease my pain somehow," Evil said and smiled his devilish grin, looking just like his father.

Z.B raised his gun and fired, aiming for Evil fast, but it was hard to see as he moved side to side. The matchet spin throws the air and slams into Z.B thigh, jamming deep inside and the blade hanging out the back of his leg.

"Ahhhh!" Z.B screamed as he tried to pull the machete out, but it was stuck in the muscle of his thigh.

Evil ran up to him and knocked the gun out of his hand. Then punched Z.B in the face repeatedly.

"I'm going to take my time with you. There is something about you I just don't like," Evil said as he knocked Z.B to the ground.

His leg was weak, and he could barely stand anyway.

"Go! Go!" Dutch said.

Tymack started to climb the faded yellow ladder, and Dutch was behind him.

"Where do you think you both are going? You'll be added to my collection. I'll keep you alive for fucking years. You belong to me.

This is what he wanted me to be, so be it. This is who I am. The son of Black ice. The son of the devil! There is no such thing as an alive and happy ending, just pain and hurt. Now all of you feel my pain." Evil said while tears streamed down his face as he thought of his wife Envy and Black ice flashbacks holding her detached head by her hair.

Evil drops to his knees. Baby. he sobbed. Then he snapped out of it when he heard Z.B screaming.

"Wait! Don't leave me! Don't leave me with this crazy fool, he's going skin me alive. Please! Tymack, help me." Z.B shouted while crying and crawling toward the wall.

 Evil stood up and kicked Z.B in the face with his size 13 timberland boot. Then, knocking him unconscious,, then started climbing the ladder.

Tymack looked down and could see Evil right behind Dutch and start kicking down and kicking Dutch hands.

"Wait, what are you doing?" Dutch said as one of his hands slipped off the ladder.

"I'm giving myself time. If he's busy killing you, I'll get the fuck away," Tymack shouted.

"No, you're wrong. You won't get out of here alive without me; I noticed something you didn't. So don't do this," Dutch plead.

"Fuck you nigga," Tymack shouted and kicked at him again.

Dutch looked down then saw the vent on the side; he leaned to the side, popped open the vent gate, and started climbing in. He made it just in time as Evil grabbed his left foot.

"Get off me! Get off me!" Dutch screamed and wiggled his foot free and crawled into the vent.

The duct vent was tight but more than enough for Dutch; he was slim built. He laid on his back and looked down and could see Evil peeking his head in, but he knew he wouldn't fit; Evil's broad shoulders would never squeeze through the vent opening—Dutch smiled.

"Don't fucking smile; you have nowhere to go; you got to come out eventually, and all add you to my collection," Evil said, then pulled his head out the duct vent.

Dutch turned back around on his hands and knees and started crawling.

"I'm getting the fuck out of here; God, please keep me safe. Thank you for taking me this far, lord." Dutch said to himself, then reached a part in the duct vent where he could crawl up, down, or go left. He started to crawl upward.

"I'm getting the hell out of here." Dutch said.

Tymack reached the door hatch in the ceiling. He twisted the yellow handle, pushed it open, and started climbing up.

"Yes," he said as he made it up into a different level and was now in the warehouse. He looks down to see Evil on the ladder smiling.

"I guess you won't be part of my collection," Evil said.

189

"No, the fuck I won't, and I'll be back pussy with why more men, don't care how good you are, I'll bring hundred African here. We'll get you," Tymack said and slammed the hatch down, then pulled the yellow handle, locking it.

"Bitch ass nigga." Tymack said, then looked around.

He could tell he was in the warehouse. But the smell of feces and urine was strong. The area was dark, and he stepped in a pile of shit. He could hear the groans of a woman in pain. He walks toward it sound.

 Dutch had climbed up and was now looking through a vent gate; he could see Tymack walking in a large room that wasn't too dark.

"You fucking asshole." Dutch mumbled, then got quick as something ran past the vent gate, then he could see red eyes way back on the far side of the room.

"Oh shit! Oh, fucking shit, it's another feeding room," Dutch said and panicked.

"Get out of there! Get the hell out of there now! It's a feeding ground! Get out!" Dutch shouted. But he's voice didn't travel well because he was on the vent.

Tymack could hear the woman crying. He moved closer to it, to see a heavy-set woman lying on her back. She looked to be 600 pounds; she was white with black hair.

"What the fuck is this? Who are you?" Tymack, asked.

The woman looked at him while crying.

"They're eating me; they're eating me," The woman said.

Tymack could hear chewing sounds coming from behind him, but he couldn't see. So, he walked around and looked, and his eyes opened wide as he saw ten baby hyenas ripping pieces of the back fat and side of the woman.

"What the fuck is going on," Tymack said as he backpedaled and could hear Dutch's voice; he turned around and ran toward it.

He ran to the far side of the room and bent down at the air vent on the floor.

"Hurry! Hurry open the vent," Dutch said as he pushed it, but the vent didn't open.

"It is welded shut. Help me! Help me! Get it open," Tymack said, then heard laughter behind him. He turns around to see four hyenas the size of a small horse.

 "What the fuck are those? What are they?" Tymack said with his voice quivering.

He stood open and took off running but didn't get far as the hyenas snatched him up and started to rip his arms and legs off.

"Please help me! Ahhhh! No!" He hollered at the top of his lungs in agonizing pain as he was eaten alive.

Dutch watched in horror, then jumped as a hyena looked through the vent gate at him and started laughing.

CHAPTER 9

The van pulled up to a house in LongIsland; Faith hopped out with Evan in her arms, Michael and Envy's two-year-old son and walked to the white house that had bars in the windows and doors.

 The front door was opened, and a brown-skinned woman holding a short barrel shotgun stood at the door.

Faith look at her and could tell Michael had her whole face, more than their father.

"You must be Rachel, your son have your face. Have you heard from him yet? I still need his help," Faith said as she passed the baby to her.

Rachel looked Faith up and down.

"I'll pray for you but I know it's to late, I can feel the devil in you already and you're set in your ways. My son Michael is no more, he's lost to me, lost to God.

I know it because he would never leave his son any where. My is baby broken, I'll pray my chocolate baby finds God and his strength once more, to pray once more but I can feel it in my belly, he's not the same." Rachel said while trying not cry.

"Thank you for bringing me my grand baby but now get off my property, before I kill you where you stand," Rachel said.

"What did you say to me?" Faith asked not believing her ears.

"You heard me bitch," Rachel said and aimed for Faith's head.

"I know how to kill the devil and his damn children, I bet if I blow your head off with this shotgun, there will be no saving you. I can feel the bad energy coming off you, bad vibes. You're toxic and don't even know it. You let him in your heart already, I raise Michael not to hurt others, to touch the world but don't let it touch him, but he did.

The loss of his wife is going be a pain too much for him to bare, but you, you enjoy killing and just a matter of time before you embrace it even more just like my son did.

Honestly all of you need to die, you'll do more harm on this earth than good, you all take more innocent souls hell. Even though I don't like you, I hope you get you're children back, no mother should be apart from there child. Fight you're hardest to get them back.

I'll send you the number to another one of your siblings that can help, his name is Bless, because I don't think Michael would be any help, he's liable to try to kill you if anything. I'll pray for you, now leave." Racheal said and entered her house and slammed down the gate shut.

Faith stood there in shock and turned around then walked back to the van.

She sat down in the passenger seat.

"Any good news?" Janice asked.

"No, Michael is still missing and Zaira hasn't tried to reach out to me yet, and I need them both, it's just you, me and Mike," Faith said as she looked at back of the van at Mike, than Taz and Egypt.

"That is not going be enough I don't know what to do, then my father won't help. We only have maybe twenty henchmen that are loyal to me. The rest is in Lefty's control, but if they see my father, this all would be over with, but he's on some I need to learn to handle my problems by

myself, to stand on my own, what type of bullshit is that.

They have your grandchildren. He wants me to run things like he would with more fear, I'm just stressed and losing hope, feel like I have no one, to one to help me, no one to watch my back. I just want my babies back." Faith said and tried not to cry.

"Bitch that is not true, I'll die for you and we will be more than enough, you're strong, stronger than any of the children your father have, that why you run things, no matter what come at us, we will win.

`
Let's get your children back and make Lefty pay for his betrayal. You have never been a weak bitch and never will, and if you're family can't come through then fuck them," Janice said then rolled up a blunt, and lit it.

"Should I be smoking with him in the back of the van, he's going get high like a motherfucker," Janice said, causing Faith to laugh.

"I just texted my older brother, he said we should met him and his wife at the private airport in twenty minutes, him and his wife will help." Faith replied.

"Michael, I thought he went missing, it's been two days, one of the henchmen said he might have taken over one of Black ice second compound in New Jersey's that had hyenas breeding in," Janice said as she passed Faith the blunt.

"No, it seems that Black ice just can't keep it in his pants because there is a lot more siblings I don't know about, but Bless is supposed to be the oldest but he's not but I heard about him, my father mostly talk about his wife and her team, The Teflon Divas, women assassins. It's supposedly where the idea for our bulletproof body suits came from and the weapons we have that got magnets in them and the formula Red velvet had stolen from them," Faith said.

"Shit, I still can't believe Red velvet grimy lazy ass was part of a women's assassin group," Janice said.

"Yeah, me too," Faith said and looked out of the window and could see Racheal peeping through her window blinds, looking at them.

"Girl pull off before Michael mother starts shooting at us. She scares me for some reason, she prays a lot and uses the bible scriptures, I'm not even scared of those catholic anointed people. But she scared me, it's something about her, as if she isn't all there." Faith said as Janice pulled off.

"Oh yeah, I found out what the real reason the catholic church is after us. It was in Josephine's journal," Faith said while passing the blunt back to Janice.

"So, what is the real reason." Janice asked.

"It's all about those books my father had in the house, the Devil Bible, and the voodoo books. Those two. back in the day slave masters part of *the catholic church use the rituals in the books to do sacrifices, killing black people, in return, they got health and wealth. They didn't know Josephine could read, she did her own ritual, killing most of them, and had a slave run away with her children and the books.*

The catholic church has been looking for our bloodline ever since and looking for the books, now my father got the books, I was told not to let him get them but they are his any way, he has them.

What change? Is question I ask myself. I just know I refuse to let the anointed people get their hands on it. They killed so many blacks people." Faith said.

"So, we got to kill lefty and Sabrina, and we need to stop them as well?" Janice asked.

"Yep and I know where to find their base, when it's time," Faith said as they pulled up to the private airport and waited as a black jet landed.

The doors opened and Faith stepped out, she could feel her brother before he step out.

The energy was different, not like Michael, Mike or Black ice, not as dark.

Bless stepped out of the jet, he was tall dark-skinned, with muscles and had a du-rag on.

"One thing about your daddy, he makes some sexy sons, but they are all shaped like him, shit he's taller than Michael but they could be almost twins and they come with those wide ass shoulders, but I'll give his sexy chocolate ass some pussy in a heartbeat," Janice stated.

"You're just a freak, but don't say that around his wife I really need their help plus from the stories she's a real bad ass, supposedly give us a run for our money in hand to hand combat." Faith replied as dark-skinned short beautiful woman exited after Bless then another dark-skinned woman with short hair and a girl that looked Chinese and black.

They walked over to Faith and Janice. Faith stared at Bless.

"I'm Faith," she said.

"I knew who you were before I saw you, I felt you," Bless replied.

"This is my wife Tess, and part of her team, the one with the short hair is Harmony B and the next is Su-young." Blessed replied.

"Hmm Red velvet really gave away our technology and more I see," Harmony said as she studied the suit that Faith and Janice had on.

"It matches theirs but ours is black and theirs is navy blue body suit. Now is not the time to have a pissing battle," Tess said looking at her, then looked at Faith.

"I agree to help you because I know what it means to have my child taken from me, my best friend took my daughter from me and killed her," Bless said

"Even though you are Black ice's daughter, you have some good in you, I can feel it and I owe Black ice a few favors, he saved me once in Detroit and captured Iris.

Have you seen her? It's been a year. Did he kill her." Tess asked.

"I have seen her maybe three times, I fought her once, she's good. My father kept her chained to a wall in a special room and told me and everyone else we're not allow to have contact with her. That she was too dangerous and smart, but I haven't seen her since my father left that compound." Faith replied.

"I thought he'll kill her by now, keeping her alive is a mistake, she will find a way to get away and I can't be looking over my shoulders," Tess said to herself.

"So, what are we up against?" Bless asked.

"As I told you before, we have to get my babies back, lefty have maybe forty henchmen and they got the catholic church after us, a group called *the anointed and the hand of God, they're like roaches, the more we kill the more keep coming, but I know what they really want beside killing all my father's children, they want what we can do,"* Faith said.

"What do you mean what you can do?" Harmony B asked.

Faith looked at her and could tell she didn't really like her.

"It's different for all of us, but we all have gifts." Faith said not saying too much about it.

"Never show your hands to people, friends or family. Make it so they won't see it coming or your next move." Black ice words played in Faith mind.

She knew the gifts all her siblings have, all of them could control animals, and Zaira could literally talk to insects, then they can all see in the dark perfectly and move in the shadows, able to travel in them and with each person they kill they get stronger, smarter.

They can sense evil, other serial killers and feel when someone from their bloodline was near by, but each family member could do something's better than others but Faith was a fast study.

She lied to Zaira and told her it was her suit that made the bugs not bite her, but the truth was she had studied her sister and learned to control the insects as well.

"Okay keep your secrets, not like it can help anything," Harmony B said then smirked.

"I'm going be honest with you, I don't like you, if you weren't family to my family I would have waited for months until you forgotten about me, and when you are sleeping, I"ll kidnap you, cut out your tongue and cut off your legs and arms and keep you alive, and I know about the healing, I have something for that as well bitch, keep up with the smart mouth. I promise you Tess or Bless won't be able to save you from me.

you better do your research. Ask them who I am, and who my father is, because clearly you don't know." Faith said while picturing chopping off Harmony B head.

"Bitch what?" Harmony said and pulled out a short sword.

Faith didn't flinch. Tess looked at Harmony.

"We're here to help, not be a problem, now is not the time for this," Tess said, knowing she trained Harmony good but if she couldn't beat Iris and Faith could, only meant one thing.

Faith was a better fighter than Harmony. Harmony backpedaled along with suyung, as they watched the large black wolf with blue eyes stare at them and walked next to Faith.

Egypt's height came up to Faith ribs. Egypt stood there snarling, showing off her long set of teeth. Faith smiled and pet Egypt on the head.

"Sit," She ordered.

Egypt sat down and kept her eyes on Harmony.

"What the hell is that?" Harmony said, never seeing a predator up close and that big.

"You have a pet wolf?" Suyung said in disbelief.

"I see you didn't tell them much at all Bless, huh. Wait to they see the hyenas but they won't be able to be good in a fight. Where we going , it's cold, so they'll move slowly unlike Egypt. Wolves are made for the cold. So is Raven!" Faith said and stretched out her arm and a black bird the size of a three year old, landed on her arms that had red eyes.

"What the fuck is that?" Harmony B said.

"This is Raven, she's a rare black hawk." Faith replied.

"She looks like she eats people," Suyung said.

"She does," Faith said with a wicked smile on her face, knowing she was telling the truth.

"Have you sent your men ahead already?" Bless asked.

"Yes and I texted Michael and Zaira, hoping they'll show up to help, I just want my kids back." Faith replied.

"We have your back. Let's get moving," Tess said as they entered the jet.

Harmony look at Mike riding on the back of Tazz,

"What fuck is that? This a damn freaky zoo, first of I have never seen dogs or wolves that big" Harmony stated.

"Have you seen many wolves up close?" Janice asked sarcastically as the plane took off.

"Tazz is a rare hyenas, and my father had most of the animals geneticallty modified, meaning they have other animals DNA inside them, some of them we know what they're mixed with and others we don't find out until they do something abnormal, but most of the hyenas grow this size, but that is nothing. I've fought and killed ones the sizes of cows and bears, those are more unstable with small brains." Faith replied.

208

"Who are these people? This is Bless sister?" Harmony said.

Su-young passed Harmony a tablet, on the screen was articles about Black ice, then she opened the government file they had on him, pictures of one of his warehouse, with babies on crack on the ground, then women skinny, looking sick, chained to the walls, and pictures of mutated hyenas in a feeding room.

"Uhmm why the hell are we helping her; her father kidnapped women, raped them and got them hooked on drugs. This some crazy shit, do you know they feed people to hyenas so there no evidence of murder, no crime." Harmony shouted.

Tess looked at her as if she was about to smack her.

"Now isn't the time to have a moral compass, we all do dirty stuff, we come from bad families, right suyung." Tess said knowing suyung's family just tried to kill them.

"We're fucking assassins for crying out loud, the Teflon divas are known killers. If my husband sister needs help than I'll help her, end of discussion," Tess said and Harmony sucked her teeth and got quite, knowing she couldn't beat Tess on her worse day.

Faith look at Bless, *"what's your real name and why doesn't Black ice talk about you or come after you like the rest of his children."* Faith asked.

"My real name is Andrew, He pretty much killed my mother, got her hooked on drugs and used to beat her. I was raised by my grandma in crown heights Brooklyn, he came for me once, when I was a teenager and said I had to much of my mother in me, I didn't see him again until I was an adult and I was hired to kill him but that didn't go so well.

I can always feel him watching me, I know when he's close by, he watches me a lot, I think he does with all his children, in a sick twisted way I think he loves us, but I wasn't part of his grand plan.

I'm not with kidnapping, and all that other stuff he's with. That how me and Michael clicked." Bless replied.

"Have you heard from him?" Faith asked.

Bless lowered his head.

"I know you heard the same thing I have been hearing. He's no longer Michael, no longer the same. He's been going around taking out crews, even women. Leaving no bodies or evidence. More than thirty-five African gangsters from New Jersey, just went missing. No clue we're they went. Story is Evil came for them, a few of them was smart enough to tell someone what was going down before they were never heard from again but he's not only killing gangsters, he picked up where Black ice left. He's killing women and kidnapping them.

The Death of his wife, really mess him up, I don't think there any getting through to him. He's most likely would try to kill us if we cross paths with him. the pain of losing someone to soon, is more than most can bare, I lost my daughter and I lost Tess and so many times she thought I was dead. That kinda pain makes you dark." Bless said.

I wanted him to face who he really was, but I didn't want him to lose himself. Not like this. I just wanted him to admit he was a killer just like the rest of Black ice children, that there was no difference just because he killed henchmen or drug dealers that he still got off on it.

Now he's completely lost. Am I to blame, maybe I could have moved faster to reach Black ice before he chopped Envy's head off, will he blame me and Zaira. Faith thought to herself as she felt Harmony B, staring at with her facial expression twisted up in attitude.

Faith close her eyes as she pictured holding her children in her arms.

CHAPTER 10

Lefty held Hope in his arms and rocked her back and forth, while humming and feeding with the bottle, he sat down on the couch inhis room and try not to think of crickets, and think of his last moment before he was killed by Michael.

He heard a knock at his door.

"Come in," He said and Sabrina stepped into the room holding Faith's son, in one hand and a cellphone on the next.

"You look sneaky, what have you been up too," Lefty asked as she flopped down next time.

"I have been working on a plan, we have twenty five of those crazy catholic Church soliders, and more suppose to come. They want Faith kids but there not going get them. We're keeping them," Sabrina said.

"You're really crazy if you think Faith or Black ice is going to let us get away with these children," Lefty said.

"I have an escape plan, that girl in Africa Mauricio, the one that got away from Faith, I called her and she said we can come there. She's safe there. Built her own army." Sabrina stated.

"Are you crazy or just stupid?" Lefty ask.

"Why do I have to be crazy because I'm not prepared to just roll over and die like you, we have more than enough men now and I have an escape plan as well. I have been one step ahead of that bitch from the beginning. She has been unable to catch me. She won't stop us. If you want to be a stupid man and give up your life because your husband died, that up to you," Sabrina said.

"Hey watch your fucking mouth, unlike you my husband wasn't a cheating bastard, he was the love of my life bitch," Lefty stated.

"So was mine but life don't stop, it keep going and so do we, one monkey doesn't stop a show." Sabrina replied.

"You're not as smart as you think you are, all that plastic surgery and you're stuck looking like an *old lady, then you lived with Black ice and Faith over a year in the compound and haven't learn much. Have you? You paid attention to the wrong things,"* Lefty said.

"How so? I was able to damn near kill her if it wasn't for you helping. So how so? Tell me," Sabrina asked.

"These babies are like magnets and GPS locations system to anyone with Black ice blood. If you pay attention. You know they can sense one another. Like if Black ice is close Faith can feel it, at first I thought it was only with him she could do that. Then the night her brothers came to Houston, and she sensed them and knew they were there.

I came to realize everyone in her family had this weird ass gift, like a GPS or warning system if you want to call it that, it was how Michael found us. Something about energy and vibes. Some bullshit. But Faith said the energy in the air change and she get a bad vibe or some kinda of feeling and she know her father close.

My point is, we can go anywhere in the damn world, if we take these babies it's like taken a homing beacon. Shinning a light saying here I am, to anyone in their bloodline that gets remotely close. So they will find us." Lefty said.

"You think too much and too negative. Like you said they have to know where to look and be close, if we're in a private island, how can they find us. They can't. We just got to go somewhere they wouldn't look, get off the grid, leave no paper trail. There are ways to live, I refuse to just give up and roll over dead." Sabrina said.

Lefty sat there and thought about what she was *saying.*

"I never really thought we can make it, I have seen the cruelty of Faith first hand. I know death will be better than letting her ever get her hands on me," Lefty said.

"You want to hurt her, that has been your goal to make her feel the same pain you feel right now. You think killing some ex-stranger brother going

make you feel better. No it is by raising her children as our own, making them take our Image, loving us and things we love, her knowing they're out there and she will never see them grow up. That will kill her. That will hurt her more than anything, she took my children from me, so I'm taking hers and keeping them and I got no plans on dying short man." Sabrina said.

"It's been two days and we haven't heard a word from her, I know she's planning something, I just wish I knew what.

Faith not stupid, Sabrina she's highly intelligent, her only weakness is she care for the people she love, but once she go dark. She's worse than her father. I seen it, She wipe out a whole fucking village in Hawaii, you should have seen it , and she did it just to get one person, she even killed children, the kids she didn't kill she sold and kept. She's ruthless when she goes dark. Why do you think she killed your family. That wasn't her, that was her when she black out and turned dark. That is what I fear right now," Lefty said.

"What can she really do to you, but kill you," Sabrina said.

"Are you fucking kidding me. Come on follow me," Lefty said as he put the baby in the crib and Sabrina did the same.

Lefty walked out his room and a henchman was standing guard.

"Look after the kids."

The henchman shook his head and enter the room.

Lefty walked to the elevator and him and Sabrina rode it down. The compound was three stories underground, like most of them with the henchmen living on the first and Lefty and Sabrina on the second.

"The last floor, is normally where the hyenas breeding project is but, Black ice didn't like the cold of Alaska too much and the hyenas didn't like it that much. That why I choose this base. It's one of the last places Faith or Black ice would

come look for us, Faith know I like to hide in plain sight so she will be looking for us in all the major cities. Her biggest mistake was letting me run everything, learn everything, stuff her father wouldn't allow. She trusted me," Lefty said.

"Yeah look what that got her, she trusted me. Thought I was an old lady and looked at me as a mother figure. She craved love, that is how she got caught sleeping," Sabrina said.

"You have to understand her, she was trapped all her life in an shitty apartment and forced to sell her body from the time she was ten, to support her mother drug habit, instead of it making her cold it made her yearn for love and a normal life and family," Lefty said.

"Yeah and the bitch thought she was going get that with my husband. I don't feel sorry for her, shit happens. She had a fucked up mother and a psychopath as a father." Sabrina replied.

"I do feel bad for her, I met Faith three years ago. I was just another henchmen, Black ice would

send groups of seven to ten men to fight Faith for her training, to push her to be better than him, at a fast pace. He was unsatisfied with the fact she didn't kill, so he told a group of us, he'll pay us three hundred dollars a piece, if we kill her during training and if we fail he was going kill us. You live with Black ice. He doesn't make idle threats. If he say he's going kill you, you're dead. It was hand to hand combat at first then he threw weapons to us. Faith killed six of the men without breaking a sweat. The last one stab her in the hand. When it came down to killing me, cricket and Jason her baby father. She refused. Even when Black ice order her too.

She said no and made us part of her personal team. The ironic thing is Black ice said we will cross her, her baby father did and so did I, I guess he was right." Lefty said as he open a room door.

"What the point of your story, you are feeling sorry and soft," Sabrina said.

"No, I just want to show you this, see Black ice collects heads and body parts. Faith does too but

221

she's a little more demonic," Lefty said as he turn in the room light.

The room was small and had a high cage in it. Inside it was four people walking on their hands and knees.

Sabrina looked closer and noticed they had no arms or legs, just hard plastic cups they used to walk on.

Two of them looked at her as Lefty pushed a bowl of oatmeal into the cage and they started fighting over it.

"This is Faith's zoo, the woman right there, that's Faith mother, she was the first to hurt and cross Faith."

"Oh my God, what did she do to her."

"She cut their tongues out, cut their limbs off, then she made sure they survived everything, gave them antibiotics and force feed them have them best doctor treat them for a month. Then

222

she stuck an ice pick into one of their ears, popping their eardrum.

So, they can't really talk and be balanced, did you know being deaf in one ear can fuck your center of gravity, Faith knows, she make sure to keep them alive, if you refuse to eat, she removes all your teeth and pump food into your stomach. The zoo is her pride and joy, she's sicker than her father.

You see the light skin guy with green eyes. That Jason her children father. Who she loved very much. You maybe asking why am I'm showing you this, it's so you'll never think she's soft.

This is will happen to us, it Faith get her hands on us. We'll become part of her zoo." Lefty said as Faith's mother stare at him and started to cry while trying to talk, Lefty knew what she was trying to say, the same thing all Black ice and Faith victims cry and beg for.

Death, they repeat the same thing.

"Kill me! Kill me."

CHAPTER 11

"Ahhh!" The henchmen tried to scream as Faith pulled him behind some trees and stabbed him in the back twice and pulled him down into the snow and lifted up his mask and sliced his neck.

North Alaska was cold with wild life everywhere, surrounded by woods, tall trees and fresh white snow on the ground than can be up to your ankles, a cold wind blow every few seconds.

Faith, Tess and the twenty henchmen she had was all dress in all white snow suits helping them blending in.

Tess stood next to Faith with a riffle in her hand, looking through the scope at the tall mountain.

"This compound is different, most of them are in homes and underground, this one inside the mountain underneath. There are always three

levels down, my children will be on the second floor.

First floor will always be the henchmen quarters," Faith said.

"I would have never thought Black ice would have such a sophisticated damn operation going on, I knew he kidnapped people but never knew it was so organized," Tess said.

Faith stood quite. *One thing I did learn, friends turn to enemies really fast and I can tell her how deep the organization really runs. How we sex traffic humans and sale body organs and get the rest hook on drugs. We have compounds all over. Black ice love real estate and land, just look at this place.*

Who would have thought to have a hideout in Alaska, I know why he did it, the border to Canada is right there, walking distance. Lefty thought he was smart and I'll never find him here. Faith thought to herself.

Lefty looked down at Hope sleeping in the crib, swaddled up, wrapped like a burrito.

Lefty smiled at the fact she was turning darker in complexion.

"Thank Allah you won't be light skin like your punk ass daddy, I'm sorry you have been going through this. Never really had any time in your mother's arms kiddo, just so much shit been happen back to back with no breaks, from the time you were cut out of her.

I pray to Allah your life doesn't always be this difficult little one and you don't see the things I have seen and that you never know what it means to find true love just to lose it. I hope and pray you know what a normal life will be like but I doubt it. We live in a crazy world, believe or not." Lefty said as his room door was bust open, and three of the catholic anointed soldiers led by a pale freckle face ginger named Flynn. Two henchmen stood behind them with there guns aim at their back.

"What is the meaning of this? Why did you bust into my room like that without even knocking, where is the fucking respect." Lefty shouted.

"There is no respect for sinners, you are not a God fearing person or you wouldn't do what you do." Flynn said sarcastically.

"Stop acting like you're any better, you kill people like I do." Lefty replied.

"Yeah, but in the name of God," Flynn stated.

"You people kill, never in history have black people massacre awhole race or killed people because they look different or have different beliefs. But guess who have? You and you all paint the history books and tell stories like you are the hero and other people fear us, grab their purse tighter.

When it was the catholic church which started the crusades killing everybody that didn't want to convert into christianity, you all wiped out the Vikings, the pagans, anyone that didn't fold under your religion, the only ones you couldn't convert was Muslim, that's why they are world's public number one enemy now, because they refuse christianity," Lefty said.

"I see you know your history unlike so many of your kind. You must be muslim Huh?" Flynn said.

"Yes I am, praise be to Allah, Allah Akbar!" Lefty said .

"We'll since you know your history you know there no beating us, besides, you ask us here to help you, if I'm correct," Flynn said.

"I didn't ask for shit, that was Sabrina, I don't trust a group a man running around in red cloaks. There's a reason the catholic church sent you all, and it has nothing to do with helping us. It's about helping yourselves," Lefty said.

"You're a smart one I see," Flynn said while walking to Lefty table.

On it was a fruit basket he took the orange out and started to peel it, throwing the orange skins on the floor.

"*I know your freckled ass is going to pack that off my floor. You got one more time to disrespect me,*" Lefty said.

Flyn smiled and waved his hand and one of his men pick the Orange skins off the floor. As he sat down in a chair by the table.

"*You're right. The church sent us here for three things. They been looking for this family bloodline for a really long time, they thought they had die off.*

As you know this Black ice and his family can do things other people can't, I heard roaches ate some of my men down to the bones because a little girl told them to? You see how valuable that is.

But they got these gifts from books they stole from us, a book of voodo and the devils Bible. So My Bishop believe if this family and bloodline is still around, then so are those books and the catholic church badly want those books, they'll move the earth to find them, so they sent me for now. To kill every member in that bloodline and take one or two of them back alive to study, my superiors are so curious of what they can do, and amazed, because just one slave was able to pull something off that would last generations. Just imagine when we can do that, after we get our hands in the books. Hmmm, truly a blessing." Flynn said while eating the Orange.

"It seems to me you're the worse evil out of them, but that doesn't explain while you are in my room uninvited, like I said I never asked for your help. Sabrina did, I don't trust you all and it seems I had every reason not to after you told me you, you're little story, my assumptions are collected." Lefty said.

"Oh, I came here for the baby girl, I'm going take her, than me and my men going leave this unholy place. This Faith is taking to long to come, eventually she'll find us if she wants her daughter and that when we will kill her, on our turf, with even more members and us having the advantage of home field," Flynn said and stood up.

"You're not taken her, over my dead body," Lefty said and pulled his gun out his hostler and aim for Flynn face.

"I wasn't asking you to give me the child, I'm ready to get out of this shit hole mountain hideout, and away from you people, this don't have to be my say, what do you people like, it's money right? We'll wire a large amount to any bank account.

This is the catholic Church, we have endless funds and resources. We can help you relocate. I see how you fear this Faith woman and Black ice," Flynn said.

"Ah ah! you people huh, you're stupid. This isn't slavery, you can't just go around and buy black babies," Lefty said.

"Yes we can, we can buy them or take them, either way, we always get what we want," Flynn replied.

"Well not this black girl, you all make the church look bad, you want to snatch or buy a baby to do

Allah know what. I can't believe it." Lefty said shaking his head.

"What is there to believe, we all got our price, even your Allah God you all worship," Flynn said.

"Allah means God, there is only one God the same God the christians and the Jews worship is the same muslims do, we just don't believe Jesus christ was God's son, he was a prophet. That the only difference, but here you are looking for the devil bible to what is really your God." Lefty said.

"The devil has always been the one and only God, everyone know it but you Jews, muslims and colored. All the celebrities and rich worship the devil, that is how they keep getting richer. It's the one thing we took from the devil bible many years ago.

Imagine what they'll learn with that book in today's day and age. How much more powerful the rich will become, God has given up on most of you along time ago, sometimes I think this is the end of days, and those faith will rule, all the lying *and deceiving will finally stop and the illuminati and new world order will just take over. Hmm one can wish."* Flynn said then looked Lefty in the eyes.

"I enjoyed this conversation with you, I didn't think someone like you can comprehend So much. I always felt your kind was simple minded," Flynn said.

"You sound real racist to be a ginger, you know ginger people come from Ireland, you're not really European like the rest of them that's why your skin is so pale and you can't deal with sun light so well.

You are supposed to be so intelligent but lack a lot of knowledge about yourself I see, how are you superior when the sun gives you cancer but doesn't harm me because of the melanin in my skin, I am letting you know black is king and we're first on this earth and always have been the superior race, you all just wrote history, as you all see fit." Lefty said.

"Enough talk, you're starting to piss me off, give me the child!" Flynn ordered.

"As I told your stupid ass, over my dead body. So make your move pussy. Fake ass catholic monkey looking ass, freckle face pussy looking ass, yellow teeth shinning like gold in your mouth but you don't have gold in your mouth ass. Fake vampire scared of the sun looking ass." Lefty said.

"Are you trying to make me even more mad?" Flynn asked.

"Yeah, so I can shoot you in your face and tell Sabrina you leaped like a frog." Lefty said, as he started to squeeze the trigger and one of his henchmen walked in the room and walked straight to him, his eyes opened up wide.

"She's here," Lefty said.

"What do you mean she's here?" Flynn asked.

"Three off the outside guards are missing. That only means one thing, Faith is here, you'll about *to learn why I'm so paranoid and fear her and Black ice.*

Just pray to whomever you pray to that she kill you," Lefty said and smirked.

"I only fear the Devil, I'm taking my men and going out there to confront this so call Faith," Flynn said as he stormed out of Lefty's room,

Lefty looked at two henchmen, get two more and you all guard Hope with your life, don't let the fake anointed soliders get any where next to her.

"I have to try to stop stupid," Lefty said then tried to catch up to Flynn.

He rode the elevator up to the main level the entry of the compound was in a cave inside the mountain. Lefty reached the top to see close to forty men dressed in red cloaks arm with military style M16 assault rifles, underneath the red cloak was army uniforms.

In front of the group was Flynn and Sabrina holding Faith's son in one of those strab on baby holder.

"This can't be good, I can feel it, maybe I should have just talked to Faith about how I felt instead of overreacting, because these people aren't with the words they say and the ground I spit on. None of them can be trusted, they have their own Agenda.

I should have seen it when Sabrina first called them, now they are about to make a stupid move without thinking or underestimating Faith. stupid fuckers."

Lefty moved past the anointed soliders with a few of his men behind him and made his way up to where Flynn and Sabrina were talking.

"What do you think you are doing?" Lefty asked.

"I'm preparing my men to go out and get that bitch, catch her alive if they can, if not we will just have to get her body." Flynn said as he gave

his men a signal and they all start existing the mountain.

"No! No this a bad idea the whole purpose of all being here was so we can have more men to fight together." Lefty said.

"Your men would only get in our way, we will get her." Flynn said without looking at him.

Lefty looked at Sabrina, *"what is your game plan or end goal Sabrina, I can understand why he's stupid and naïve but you lived with us for over a year, you know this plan is dumb, if they go looking for her instead of letting her come for us. They're asking for death."* Lefty stated.

Sabrina moved closer to him, so only him can hear, *"it will only give us more time to escape when the killing starts."* She whispered and smiled, then kissed the baby boy that was fast a sleep to the on the harness strapped to her chest on the forehead.

Lefty grabbed Flynn, *"listen you underestimate us and underestimate her. By sending your men* into those woods, you're killing them. Call them back, I'll get the rest of my men and we wait until she hit the compound. She will come, she's already here now, you have no idea what you're getting yourself into and if her siblings are with her, it's even worse." Lefty said.

Flynn pulled his arm away, "don't fucking touch me, and my race has being hunting and killing you blacks for a long time, I'm tired of you making it seem like you all are so special. You got a little money and think you all have the same influence and power we do? No sir. My men are military trained. They'll end this fast. Your men are just playing dress up, in black body suits and black mask. Just for imitation." Flynn said.

Lefty smirked, and shook his head and couldn't believe the stupidity that came out of Flynn mouth.

"Even if Faith only had her henchmen with her that still would be a problem. Each henchmen is trained in the compound everyday in weapons and hand to hand combat and their whole *uniform down to the mask was bulletproof. Only weak spot was the neck and back of the head. Black ice made sure there was no weak link they are all dead."* Lefty said and shook his head

CHAPTER 12

"Report," Flynn said into the bluetooth earpiece he had on.

"We're entering the woods now, nothing but snow out here and no foot prints yet. We sending the drones up," Luke the lieutenant of the anointed soliders said.

"Let God lead you brother." Flynn said as one of his me set up a portable table and pulled out monitor screens, and set them up.

"Faith can't beat technology, we'll be able to see everything and any moment from the sky and report back to my men. I told you this is going be fast and fun, like hunting black back in slavery," Flynn said confident.

Lefty looked at him and shook his head, but kept his eyes on the monitors watching the anointed soliders starting to go into the woods. The snow was higher in the woods, came up to there calf muscles, making it hard for them to walk, each step had to be big and wide, to get anywhere.

"The teams are breaking up to groups sir, God is with us," Luke said.

"That is not a good idea!" Lefty said.

"Shut up and don't interfere."

"You know what? I'm going sit back and watch the show, obviously you're stupid and Sabrina over here has her own agenda, cause she's not stupid," Lefty said then walk back to his men.

"She's coming, get everyone ready." Lefty said then walked back over to the monitors.

"Group A check in, any sight of moment yet?" Luke asked into his earpiece but got no answer.

"Group A this is Luke, come in, is there any sight of the target," Luke said and still got no answer.

"Flynn we lost contact with Group team A, do you see anything with the drones?" Luke asked.

"Hold on, I see you and the other teams, the trees are in the way," Flynn replied into his earpiece.

Lefty looked at Sabrina and raised his left eyebrow. Both of them knew what time it was, that shit was about to hit the fan, they had seen it too many times over with Faith and Black ice.

"Ahhhh! Ahhh! Help me! Help me!" A man could be heard screaming, and gun fire went off.

"This way!" Luke said as he took his team of anointed soliders deeper into the woods.

"Wait I see something," Flynn said looking at the monitor as the seven drones flew around.

"Our men are down. There is blood everywhere." Flynn said.

Luke and his team reached the site. The snow was turned red, anointed soliders guns and pieces of their cloak were everywhere, but there were no bodies. Just one man laying on his back, squirming around in pain.

 Luke apportioned him with a few of his men right behind him and the rest spread out? With their guns aimed high, looking for anything that was moving. There were blood trails everywhere.

"Where are the men! Where is the rest of your team?" Luke asked then noticed that the man hands had been chopped off.

"Help me! God please save me," the man said as he turned on his side and started vomiting.

"They made me swallow something, they made me swallow it." The man cried in between vomiting in the snow, green liquid mixed for food prodigals then a whole blue eyeball came out his mouth, along with a small black device.

Tess watched than smiled.

"Show time" she mumbled and then pressed a button on her watch, the black devices exploded. Blowing up three of the anointed soliders.

Faith popped up from underneath the snow from behind the anointed solider and stabbed him in the back of the head, then pulled out her gun and shot the next one on the side of his head.

Chaos broke loose as the anointed soliders fired toward her but Bless shot and killed two, and Tess jumped out of a tress and landed on one, and snapped his neck, he got up quickly and side kick another as he landed on the ground she shot him in the face.

Faith henchmen popped up and fired at seven henchmen, killing four of them.

"What going on out there?" Flynn screamed.

"They are killing us! They are fucking killing us, they're popping out everywhere, in the trees, underneath the snow, they are wearing white. We can't track them, you said they'll be untrained. They are moving like a trained unit sir. May God be with us," Luke said as he ran with five of his men by his side.

 A rope came down and wrapped around one of his men neck and harmony pulled on it and drop out of the tree, using her body weight to lift the man up, as she fell down she squeezed the trigger to her mp5 submachinegun sending a hail of bullets into two of the anointed soliders. As the other one choked and tried to get the rope off his neck but he died in seconds.

Flynn couldn't believe what was happening, he only had a few men left. He looked at Lefty to see smirking.

"You think this is funny, those are God fearing men out there dying, some scum is killing them." Flynn shouted as his face turned bright red and spit flew out his mouth.

"I warned you not to underestimate her and her family, I warned you not to go into the woods, where she would have the most advantage, we had the numbers a small army together but you fucked that up." Lefty said.

Flynn looked him dead in the eyes.

"You're a fool if you think we ever needed your help, my church run the world," Flynn said then walked back over to the monitor.

"Team B engage now," Flynn said.

Lefty looked at Sabrina with a confused look on his face as three helicopters could be heard approaching, they hovered over the woods and men in red cloaks, armed with m16 riffles zip line down.twelve snowmobiles came out of no where with two men on each one, riding into the woods firing.

Bless fired and killed three anointed soliders but more chase him in the woods, Faith was surround by ten. Luke smiled.

"They said take you alive, don't put up a fight but they said it's okay if you came in dead as well," Luke said aiming his gun at Faith head.

"They keep coming, where are they coming from" Tess shouted while ducking for cover behide a tree and four of Faith's henchmen dropped to their knees as bullets filled their bodies.

Flynn looked at Lefty.

"You didn't think we knew about your bulletproof body suit and mask the henchmen had huh, we have armor piercing bullets. It will work on any metal beside that Teflon I think Faith and Black ice and the rest of the main people suit are made of, I heard Black ice leather coat is made of

Teflon. I wonder if it's true? Is it?" Flynn asked and smirked.

Lefty stood quite and watched; the anointed was an unstoppable army.

Hope, I have to keep her safe, if they knew about our armor, that means they plan to cross the whole time, they're going try and take the twins. I can't let this man get his hands on them. I can tell he's a piece of shit. Lefty thought to himself.

"You don't have much to say Lefty, do you. You swear Faith and her people was something special. They're trained really well I must admit that but we have numbers and that is what really matters, I'll have her and her children for my Bishop. It's a good thing cause it's cold, my balls is freezing in this shit hole, unholy place," Flynn said smiling then went back at the monitors.

Suyung pulled out her staff and stabbed one of the anointed in the forehead and another on in the neck.

"Ahhh!" She screamed as bullets slam into her back but bounced off her Teflon body suit.

"Where are they coming from." Suyung said and ran to find cover, she saw Harmony and ran toward her.

"There are too many of them. We're going have to fall back," Bless said and ducked behind a tree and shooting as bullets nearly hit his skull.

Black ice and Zaira stood on a small mountain close by and could see everything clear.

"She's loosing. There are too many of those chuck guy like before in New York. They kept coming," Zaira said as her heart race.

"They want your sister and the books," Black ice said patting his inside coat pocket.

Faith looked around to see two more of her henchmen killed and everyone else ducking for cover while in a gun fires. She found herself surrounded by twenty anointed soliders.

"God love us, so we will win. There is nothing you can do, just give up now."

"Like said, Never," Faith said and shot an anointed on the head, then they rush her. She broke the arm of one and kicked another and punch another in the nose breaking it.

She fell forward as one hit her in the back of the head with the butt of his riffle. They threw a net over her as if she was a fish or wild animal and start kicking her repeatedly, and hitting her with their riffles, using their guns as baseball bats.

"Die bitch! You unholy bitch. Die, God is with us. We are the nightly, the worthy! The strong, all blessings come from him so you'll never win. We are the hand of God." The anointed soliders shouted while beating her as if they practiced saying the same thing every day.

"They got her! They're going kill her." Zaira shouted.

"We should help her, we can't let them kill her or kidnapped her." Zaira shouted.

"She's your sister, what are you going to do about it, or the bright side if she dies, I guess you'll be my favorite then," Black ice said coldly and looked down at Zaira as her mind contemplated the scenario.

"She's my sister," Zaira said.

"So was the twins you ripped out of Jadore body and kill them, they were your siblings right, I didn't put her in there for you to kill her, she wasn't the test. The little girl was, to see if you'll try to befriend her and save her like your sister did with the ones that betrayed her now. I wanted to see if you was going save that little girl, but you let her and the lady escape, now we got to find them. But that is not the problem." Black ice said in a deep dark demonic tone.

"Those little brats in that lady's belly had no connection to me. Faith my sister, she saved me

251

and trained me. I won't let her die," Zaira said and started sliding down the mountain.

Black ice smirked.

The anointed soliders stopped beating Faith and Luke walked up to her holding a long dagger.

"I heard you all heal and I was told to take your fucking head off if you give me any problems. So are you going give me problems?" Luke said.

"Fuck you!" Faith shouted.

"Hold her down I'm going saw this bitch head off," Luke said.

Seven anointed soliders held Faith down, along with the weighted net over her body it made it impossible for her to move.

"Ouch," Luke said, trying to sound manly for screaming as something bite his face.

"Ouch" he said again this time smacking himself in the face and look at his hand, blood and a squished black fly.

"What the hell. It bite me twice." Luke said then looked down at Faith smiling.

"What the hell you're smiling about. You're a dead bitch," Luke said.

"My sister is here, she came. I didn't think she'll come," Faith said then started laughing, her laughter was dark and scary. It creeped the group of anointed soliders out.

"Shut that sinner bitch up! I don't care who comes no one can stop us," Luke said.

"Then you don't know my family," Faith said while still smiling, buzzing sounds could be heard coming from every direction.

"What the hell is that? What is that sound?" Luke asked, then black clouds covered the woods and flies began to attack.

"Ahhh!" The anointed soliders began to scream as the flies bit them then others entered their mouth. They ran in circles hitting themselves, others rolling onto the snow.

Zaira rushed in and started removing the net from over Faith head, then help her kick it off.

Faith hugged her tight.

"Thank you," Faith said.

"Don't go soft on me, we're not the emotional type remember," Zaira said then smiled and hugged her back.

Their embrace was cut short as four the anointed soldiers took off their cloaks and hand backpacks full of gas connected to flame thrower.

Fire spit out and danced in the sky and made lines, as if someone was peeing, burning the flies that came in.

Zaira concentrated hard to call me more, but the anointed soliders were burning them too fast.

Flynn turned around, *"see we do our research you only get to drop on us once, then we figure out a solution real fast. they told us what this little sister could do, I didn't think it was true and wouldn't beige it, if I didn't see it with my own eyes, smart girl using genetic modified Insect, we even study the dead flies from the first house she attack us amazing specimen she got it so they eat flesh and repopulate fast. Kinda deadly what if they ever get out in the world on their own, now we have a new deadly species that pretty much can wipe out our food supplies, killing all livestock.*

That just one scenario, second one scenario. The next one is what if this Zaira just lose it and turns to an evil genius and populate enough of those damn thing to kill livestock on purpose and fruit trees. She would bring the earth to an dark age that she can control. The Bishop wants her bad, if we can mimic what she does. The church will be even more powerful." Flynn said smiling at Lefty.

"Why do you look so down, I thought you wanted us to get rid of them. That is exactly what we are doing. So don't have that face, everythjng they thought of we thought of a way to stop it. It's over for them, everyone that share that bloodline will be killed or caught. They are outnumbered and we got more technology.

Like I told you Mr. Lefty sir. The babies are coming with us and you all can never beat the anointed soliders, we're the hand of God," Flynn said feeling confident and cocky, knowing he had won already.

Black ice looked down from the mountain he was at and shook his head in disbelief, then turned around and walked down. He reached a secret door on the mountain he was on and opened it.

Growling could be heard then laughter. He grinned his devilish smile as he looked at hundreds of red growling eyes staring back at him.

Luke took one of the backpacks, after smacking himself in the face again. He walked over to Faith and Zaira.

"Do you know how much it hurt when those things bite you? We'll do you?" Luke shouted.

"Well yes, we have all been bitten by Zaira's flies," Faith said sarcastically.

"I really don't have to take back both of you alive, infact they want the little girl more because of the bugs." Luke said then an anointed solider threw a net on Zaira from behind her, then hit her on the back of her head. She fell to the ground, and groaned in pain and the flies started fading away.

"Now you!" Luke said and aimed the flamethrower at Faith.

"I'm going burn you to a crisp then chop of your unholy head for the bishop," Luke said as he started to squeeze the trigger of the flamethrower.

Raven flew down and hovered in front of Luke blocking him from getting to Faith. She then attacked Luke, using her razor sharp claw to scratch his face then his left eye.

"Ahhhh! You fuck animals!" Luke hollered in pain and squeezed the trigger to the flamethrower, setting Raven on fire.

She hovered for a second, looking like a Phoenix as she screamed and hit the ground.

The smell of burnt flavors and chicken linger in the air. Raven was still moving a little as Luke held his eye with one hand and aimed down and squeezed the trigger to the flamethrower once more and burnt Raven alive, killing her.

"Nooooo! Nooo!" Faith screamed and dropped to her knees, while looking at Raven's body burn.

Raven has been her protector and guardian her baby for three years. She raised her when she was no bigger than the size of her hand. Tears streamed down her cheeks as flashbacks played in her mind of all the people she lost and unable to hold her babies and now Raven.

Black ice left the door opened and returned to the top of the mountain. He looked and could see everything clear. The battle that was still going on, with the anointed outnumbering Faith and her siblings, then he saw Faith on her knees.

"Show them! Show them why you're my fucking favorite and get the fuck up!" Black ice said in a dark tone and Faith looked in his direction as if she could hear every word he said.

 It was the same words he said when he was training her. Faith looked at her father and than screamed.

"Ahhhhhh!" At the top of her lungs, the sky went dark and buzzing sounds could be heard.

"Stop that! Knock her back out." Luke said noticing Zaira was getting back up.

Zaira looked confused, *"that is not me, I'm not doing that."* Zaira said to herself while still trapped in the net on the ground, she turned her head and looked at Faith screaming.

"It's her, she's doing it. She could control them all along." Zaira mumbled to herself then remember how the insects would attack all her siblings, but never Faith, then Zaira remembered the number one rule Faith told her.

"Never show anyone your hand, not even friends or loved ones. She never showed me her whole hand." Zaira thought to herself and smiled.

But then the sound of footsteps charging toward the woods could be heard, sounding like a stampede.

"What the fuck is going on here?" Flynn asked with a confused look on his face as he went to the front of the cave entrance and looked at the dark sky and black clouds that came out of

nowhere and could hear the ground rumbling. He looked at Lefty for answers.

"You pissed off the devil's daughter, honestly I wouldn't want to be you or your team right about now," Lefty said and smiled with a sarcastic look on his face.

CHAPTER 13

Flynn went back to the monitor, to look at the drone but could barely see anything.

"What's that noise. What aim I hearing." Flynn shouted.

As the buzzing sound grow louder, Mike went over to Tess, and looked up at the trees.

"Tell them to get in the tress now." Mike said as everyone stopped shooting and started looking around.

Faith screams echoed through the woods. Her pain and sadness then rage, could be felt through everyone body.

"Climb the trees now." Tess told her team and the henchmen that was left on Faith team.

"What the hell is she?" Harmony asked as she sat on a branch up in a tree and flies, mosquitoes nd beatles swarmed in groups of millions.

The ground began to tremble and felt like an earthquake.

"What the hell is going on?" Luke said and turned around and could see something running toward them.

"Fire! Fire! Shoot you fools! Shoot!" Luke shouted but it was hard to hear him over ther buzzing sounds and of a stampede.

Genetic altered albino hyenas, 4 feet tall charged into the woods and snatched up the anointed soliders, and started eating them.

"What the hell are they?" Luke screamed as a man next to him got grabbed and four hyenas ripped him apart and started laughing while eating.

"Shoot them, shoot them!" Luke shouted.

They aimed and fired, killing seven of them but more was coming.

"Ahhhh!" Faith screamed louder and the flies and mosquitoes and beetle started to attack the anointed as well, making it hard for them see, they tried to burn them but then forgot about the hyenas and got snatched.

"No! No," an anointed solider screamed while faning the flies off then ran into a tree because he couldn't see. He laid on his back and smiled because the bugs were no longer biting him.

Then, he felt drool drop on his forehead and lips. He looked to the see razor sharp teeth smiling down at him, before he could scream, his head was ripped off and hyenas started to fight over his body laughing.

Bless was in a tree next to his wife Tess, looking in disbelief.

"How is she doing this?" Tess asked.

"I don't know baby , but I think she really didn't need anyone's help. She just wasn't as pissed off as she thought she was. Because she's mad now, I think we should stay in these trees for a while." Bless replied.

 Then looked and could see Black ice standing on a mountain with his machete in his hand, just watching everything.

"That is it girl, show them all, show them you're not weak, show them you're the devil's daughter. Show them chaos! Show them why you're my fucking favorite!" Black said with an evil smirk on his face and knew that Faith could somehow hear him.

Faith stopped screaming and stood up. She reached behind her back and pull out her double edged ax, her father gifted her and started swinging, chopping the head of one of the anointed soliders, then ran to Luke and kicked him on the back, Luke stumbled forward and turned around.

He squeezed the trigger of the flamethrower, flies and bugs jumped in front of Faith and acted as a shield as they burnt to a crisp. Faith moved to the side and cut the hose that connected the backpack to the flamethrower. Luke noticed that it wasn't working after he squeezed the trigger twice, he took the backpack off and held his long dagger in his hand.

"You're doing all of this somehow bitch, ain't you? This why the Bishop wants you alive, but you killed too many of my men. I'm going chop your head off and I bet all of this this will end," Luke said as hyenas ran past him and attacked his men.

He swung at Faith, she dropped her ax and grab his arm in mid-swing. He looked at her and knew he was stronger and tried to push his hand down to stab her in the chest but his hand didn't move.

"How is she so strong." Luke said.

Zaira took the net over her head, *"rule two never let them know how physically strong we really are. Never use your full strength the formula make us stronger than three men. But you must always keep that secret until it's time."*

Faith words played in her mind.

"This is what she meant." Zaira said to herself.

Faith twisted Luke's arm, breaking it.

"Ahhhh! Ahhh!" He screamed in agonizing pain and started to cry. Faith kicked his leg, making him fall to the ground, then she hopped on the ground with him and twisted his left ankle.

"Ahhhh! Stop! God protect me! Help me!" Luke cried out as Faith took his right ankle and twisted it, breaking it.

"Ahhh stop please don't! No more! No more!" Luke cried out as a huge albino hyena came up on him. he stopped screaming as he study the animal teeth and big mouth.

Faith got up off the ground as Egypt ran to her side.

Faith looked at the hyena, *"take him and don't kill him, no one eats him,"* Faith said.

Luke eyes opened wide as the hyena's mouth stretched open wide and he bit Luke on the shoulder and dragged him away.

"Help me! Please help me! Some one anyone help me! I can't die like this! Not like this!" Luke cried out as he was drag through the snow and he felt as if everything was moving in slow motion.

He could see the hyenas eating his men, then shooting a few of them but more and more kept coming.

"Where are they coming from?" One of the anointed soliders shouted while trying to run in the snow, each step he took was harder than the next, he stopped as he was surround by twelve hyenas.

He heard a noise and looked up to see Harmony and suyung in the trees high up. He ran toward a tree and start climbing it as fast as he could. A hyena ran and leaped in the air and yanked him off the tree.

"Oh shit!" Harmony said as they hyena start to rip his legs off and fought over them.

The anointed soliders crawled while they fought over his legs and thigh.

He looked up at harmony.

"Please help me! Help me! I don't want to die. Not like this! Not like this!" The anointed solider cried, then he stopped crying as his body quivered. He could feel the hot breath of a hyena breathing on the back of his neck, standing over on him. The hyena bit his shoulder and turned him over onto his back and started to laugh.

"Hahah! Hahah!" His creepy laughter of excitement cause more hyenas to come over.

They surround the anointed solider as he laid on his back with no legs, praying to bleed out.

"Please God let me die before they get me. Please let me go to sleep. Lord here my praise. I am the hand of God. Please help me," The anointed soliders prayed out loud but his prayers went unheard as the hyena ripped open his stomach and started eating him, then the others got excited and started laughing and ate his arms then his face.

"Oh, damn!" Suyung said as she looked down from the tree with harmony B, as the snow turned deep red.

Faith hopped onto Egypt back and the flies and bugs start to go away, and thirty of the albino hyenas followed her as she rode toward the mountain.

 Lefty shook his head as he watch all the chaos and mayham most of the anointed soldiers were dead, being eating and only a few were left but was out number and overwhelmed by the hyenas.

Lefty could see Faith riding toward them and would be at the cave at any second.

"I told you not to underestimate her. You did and now you're looking stupid," Lefty said as he watched Faith ride toward them.

He didn't hear a smart replied from Flynn he turned around to see that Flynn was gone and so was Sabrina.

"Oh shit, Hope!" Lefty said and noticed the henchmen behind him were dead with bullet holes through their face mask.

"How didn't I hear this. They must have used silencer," Lefty said as he pick up a mp5 machine gun from one of his dead henchmen and took off running down the cave, as he was running he saw dead bodies of henchmen.

Fuck Sabrina double crossed me. I knew I couldn't trust that bitch. She was always out for herself and I should of listen to my gut when she first involve the catholic church with these so called anointed soliders, she's always planning the best outcome for herself. She doesn't care about anyone but herself, so why shouldn't I think she would double cross me. Lefty thought to himself.

As he ran inside the cave and rode the elevator down. He stopped on the first floor to see most of his henchmen dead, beside four.

"What happen here?" Lefty asked.

"Flynn and the few guard he has caught us off guard with armor piercing bullets, they killed everyone and Sabrina was with them," One of the henchmen said.

Lefty looked at all the henchmen's dead body and shook his head.

"You four come with me now," Lefty said and they hopped in the elevator, and rode it down to the second floor.

As soon as the elevator stopped. Lefty knew something was wrong. The smell of death was in the air, along with feces and urine.

When people die they lose control of their bowels and shit on themselves, no matter how hard they try not to. It always happens.

Lefty walked out the elevator with his gun drawn and the henchmen behind him, he walked down the hallway to his room to see the four henchmen that were guarding Hope was dead.

He entered his room to see Flynn holding Hope and anointed soliders with him.

"I told you, the church never lose, we lost the battle but we didn't lose the war. We'll collect all the data that happen here today and she will be unable to get the drop on us. You was right Lefty we underestimate her and the situation. I thought it was going be much easier but she surprised me.

Sabrina didn't tell me everything and where did all those hyenas come from. There clearly stuff we don't know. You said the hyenas don't like the cold but those beast outside are running around like they're at home," Flynn said.

"Black ice keep a lot of secrets just like Faith, but I warn you this was a loosing battle, now put down Hope," Lefty said.

"That's what you all name her. Hope. It sounds very catholic and Christian. That a good name." Flynn replied.

"I guess, but she was named Hope because when she get her hands on you, you'll lose all hope. Kind of like Faith, she will test your faith in whatever God you people believe in. I don't even think you all will be alive Allah. You cried all the time," Lefty said.

"Our God is the one true God and you all made me disappoint him twice today. But that doesn't matter right now. I have hope, my Bishop will be

pleased to see her and cut her open and study her," Flynn said.

"They say we are the monsters and bad guys but listening to you, make me sick, you all are using the church bas a weapon, just for power and fast kill, yet call yourself holy, half of you don't even know which God you worship, your soliders don't know you all really pray to the devil, everything about you all is wrong. Now, Put the baby down and let's finish this." Lefty said, wanting to shoot Flynn in the face but couldn't because he was holding Hope.

"Anyone ever told you, that you talk a lot Lefty and your words hurt, you're a very annoying guy. I'm going spit in your face after I kill you. Today have been a trying day, I'm frustrated I even have to be here. So let's get this shit over with," Flynn said and the lights went out.

Hope started crying louder and gun fire, lit up the dark room. Lefty held his fire, and then bent down and shot Flynn in the thigh.

"Ahhh!" He screamed in pain and took off, lefty follow the sounds of Hope crying. He stopped for a brief second to look back to see two of his henchmen were dead but they had killed all the anointed soliders.

"Motherfuckers was never trained better than us. They just had armor piercing bullets and caught us off guard and they had the numbers, more men. Thats' it. All that shit Flynn said was just talk."

Flynn ran down the hallway and saw the elevator come down, the door open to Faith standing there with Egypt her black wolf standing by her side. Footsteps could be heard on the top floor, letting him know that the hyenas had gotten into the compound.

"You have no where to run! Give up the child now." Lefty shouted as he exit the room, He didn't even see Faith as he chased Flynn.

"You better not hurt her! I'll fucking kill you!" Lefty shouted.

Flynn ran toward the staircase door and went through it. He could hear laughter and footsteps on the top floor then he could see two albino hyenas.

"Fuck! What's up with this place, why do they have those things running around loose," Flynn said as he held his leg where lefty shot him and Hope in his arm and tried not to drop his gun as he limped down the stairs to the third floor.

"Flynn! Give me back my baby! Give up my niece you ass hole. I promise I'll let you leave here with your life." Lefty shouted as he ran into the stairwell and stopped as two albino hyenas stared at him then one leaped to attack.

He squeezed the trigger to mo5 machine gun. Filling the hyena chest full of holes while it was in the air, killing it. The second one stood by the top of the stairs and made a funny sound. A sound Lefty already knew what it was. He was calling for backup and more help.

"Oh shit, not today, not now!" Lefty said as he ran down the stairs.

These hyenas are wild, and why are they white, Black ice must have breed them himself. Made a breed that can withstand the cold but kept them isolated, making them even more Savage. The other hyenas never attack the henchmen, it's like they can smell Black ice or Faith on us. Only those freakish monster hyenas Black ice fed fat women filled of steroids, their brains are small, but these are smarter. He literally just called for help. I'm going have to find away to get pass them once I get Hope. But let me handle one problem at a time. That's getting my niece back. I went about all of this the wrong way because of my pain and lost, now looking at me, I'm being hunted by albino hyenas, while chasing a lieutenant to a catholic church cult. Yeah, my life really went to shit, Lefty thought to himself.

Flynn made to the third level of the compound, he ran down the hallway and there was only one door? He opened it and ran inside.

The room was huge and designed to make you think you were outside in a jungle. Even the humility asw high, making Flynn instantly start sweating.

Trees were everywhere and plants with big leaves, tropical birds, birds the color of red and blue and yellow was in the trees. The sound of a owl making noise could be heard.

"How the hell am I in a rainforest. They built this in here. Why? And how big is it," Flynn said to himself as he walked deeper in and felt like there was no end to the room, but no longer felt like he was being chased.

He stopped and sat on a rock and removed his red cloak and placed it on the floor, then placed Hope, who was fast asleep in her swaddle in it.

Flynn ripped his cloak and tied a piece of it around his thigh, putting pressure on his bullet wound.

"Shit burn. No one never tell you how much it actually burn getting shot. I can't stand that

short bastard Lefty" Flynn said out loud to himself.

"Well the feelings mutual." Lefty said and sent two bullets toward Flynn head.

Flynn mange to duck the shots and crawl behind the rock he was sitting in.

"You son of a bitch!" Flynn shouted.

"You have such a horrible mouth for a man of God, you've been cursing like a sailor since you got here. Fuck this! Asshole that! Like who raised you. That is as far as your vocabulary goes? you're one of those people that like to pretend they're intelligent but really not, just memorized a few lines from books. Then walk around like you all superior and better than everybody else because deep down you know you slow and stupid.

I bet you can't even read an urban novels I like to read. I see right through you Flynn, The fake confidence the fake tough guy act. I know your really a bitch. I see it." Lefty said while hiding behind a tree.

"Fuck you lefty! You short bastard!" Flynn said, then laughter started echoing through out the room.

"You said that already and those weird albino hyenas, follow me here I think they hunting me and you. So we only got a few seconds to finish this shit up. They're not normal hyenas. These things are smart and vicious at the same damn time. I'm pretty sure they're going eat me and you. I can see it happening." Lefty said with a smirk on in his face.

"Ahahah!" Laughter could be heard along with movement directly behind Flynn he turn around and fired two shots into the moving bushes.

Lefty took off running like a football player and grabbed Hope off the ground and turned around and took off.

Flynn turn back around.

"You fast bastard," and squeezed the trigger, a bullet slam into Lefty back and pierced through the armor of his body suit and and came out the front of his stomach.

Lefty coughed up blood and continue to run.

As Flynn fired again shooting him on the back of the thigh, Lefty tripped and fell, making sure not land on Hope as he hit the gun and his gun fell out his hand into the bushes somewhere.

"I really don't understand you, you're such a weird short guy. You cross your friend, fed us information, but protect her child, don't want to give it up. When you're the one that kidnapped her in the first place." Flynn said as he walked up to Lefty on his stomach holding onto Hope.

"Call me crazy but I rather die protecting this baby my niece, over giving it to some crazy catholic church people. What are you all really going do to a black baby. Nothing nice I can bet on that. So no I'm not going give her to you.

I crossed Faith but she's still the sister I never had. Family fights, I threw a temper tantrum and willing to die for it. But I'm not willing to give you this child," Lefty said.

"That okay, because you're going die and I'm still going get that baby" Flynn said.

"How?" Lefty said knowing that they were surrounded.

"How the hell are you going get out," Lefty said while laughing and Flynn shot him in the ass, then looked around and he could see red eyes staring at him from the dark jungle and movement all around him.

Flynn fired in the woods and he saw some of the eyes close shut, letting him know he killed two or three. He heard a clicking noise, letting him know he was out of bullets.

"Now isn't the time for the bullshit," Flynn said as he got scared and could hear more movement then felt something sting him in the neck. Lefty

turned around to see Flynn pull a dart out of his neck. He look down at lefty.

"What the fuck is this?" Flynn asked.

"Oh you're in for one hell of surprise when you wake up, I remember those darts." Lefty said.

"What do you mean when I wake up," Flynn replied as he felt like he was spinning in a circle and he could see the albino hyenas step out, their red eyes looking at him then he saw Faith step out and pet one of them on the head and shot him with a dart gun in her hand as he collapsed and lost consciousness.

Lefty looked up at Faith and stretched his arm out and passed her Hope.

"By any chance can you kill me fast?" Lefty asked and closed his eyes and felt a dark needle hit his hand.

"I guess not," he replied.

"Where is my son Lefty?" Faith said in a stern tone.

"Sabrina got him, she's trying to escape with the anointed, something about a helicopter waiting a mile from here, that this asshole supposed to catch if he got his hands on Hope but I wouldn't let him, I wouldn't let him Faith," Lefty said sounded intoxicated, his words were slurry as he went to sleep, knowing when he open his eyes things would be worse.

CHAPTER 14

———— ❧ ————

Sabrina looked back while on the snowmobile, she could see Bless and Tess chasing her, somehow they mange to steal a snowmobile from two anointed soliders and got passed the crazy wild hyenas and was on Sabrina and three anointed soliders ass.

Tess jumped off her snowmobile and hopped onto Bless's and stood up and fired, shooting one of the anointed in the back of the head, his snowmobile twisted and turned then flipped over and exploded.

"Damn woman I love watching you work, Bless said as he got turned on.

Tess smiled.

"You haven't seen nothing yet husband." Tess replied seductively, as an anointed solider fired back at them. Bullets slammed into her chest but bounced off her body armor.

"Fuck," Tess said as she sat down for a second, and held Bless tight.

"You okay baby,"

"Yeah, I'm good but those armor piercing bullets don't work on my bodysuit but they hurt like hell, knock the wind out of me." Tess replied.

"No one hurts my wife," Bless said as he speed up and pulled out his 50 caliber desert eagle handgun and fired.

The large bullet spent in the air and slammed into the back of the head of the anointed soliders, blowing off half of his face, his snowmobile slammed into a tree. He was dead long before then. Bless aimed at the last one and shot him in the back, killing him instantly, then he aimed at Sabrina's back as she rode her snowmobile.

"No don't, the bullet will go through her and hit the baby, you can't risk that," Tess said, reminding him, how powerful his gun was.

Bless aimed and shot out the snowmobile tracks.

"No! No!" Sabrina said panicking.

She could see the helicopter with anointed soliders in it but the snowmobile started smoking and stopped.

"We got you!" Tess said as they pulled up on her, bullets slammed their snowmobile

"Jump off." Bless shouted.

They leaped off into the snow as it exploded, then a flash grenade went off blinding them for a second.

Bless opened his eyes to see his brother, putting Sabrina and the baby on his Snowmobile.

"Michael what are you doing?" Bless shouted.

"I'm going to hurt that bitch and my father like they hurt me." Michael replied.

"But their your family, that baby is your nephew, he's innocent." Bless shouted.

"No one's innocent Bless, you should know that and my name is Evil. If I see you again I will kill you," Michael said and took off.

He made it to the helicopter and help Sabrina into it and he climbed in.

Tess look up and could see Mike tied up and the anointed holding him down with a net covering his body as the helicopter flew away.

"I think we going have to kill your brother baby." Tess said.

"No I'll leave that to Faith." Bless replied and shook his head.

CHAPTER 15

Zaira stood next to Black ice back on the mountain and watched the helicopter fly away.

"What do we do now?" Zaira asked.

"We free your brother Mike and get your nephew back. No matter the cost," Black ice said as he touched the book inside his coat pocket.

"What about Michael?" Zaira asked.

"Leave him to me," Black ice said and walked off.

Zaira stood on the mountain watching the albino hyenas eat anointed soliders and all the snow in the woods was mostly deep red.

Luke woke up strapped to a cold steel table. Butt naked. His head was strapped down as well. He only could move his eyes. He looked over and could see Flynn asleep in a table next to him.

"Sir! Sir wake up." Luke shouted as his body trembled in fear.

"Get up!" Luke screamed as Faith walked in the room with a woman dressed as a nurse and two henchmen, one holding a small blowtorch.

"Good you're up," Faith said.

"What are you going to do to me? please I'll tell you anything, I'll tell you where our base is at," Luke said.

"I already know where it's at. You killed Raven, she was like a child to me. I raised her, she was a gift from my father and she was one of a kind, there are more hawks but not like her. My father gave her human intelligence. I loved her," Faith said trying not to cry.

"So, I'm going add you to my zoo, you'll be my new pet while I try to figure out how to make another Raven, when I do I'll have to train it all over again. But then I'll let her eat you. That is when you'll die," Faith said as she pulled out her hatchet from the hostler on her thigh and swung, chopping off Luke's right arm from the joint then a henchmen heated up a machete and pressed it against the wound.

"Ahhhghhh! Ahhh!" Luke screamed as his body trembled, before he could recover from the pain

Faith swung again and chopped off his right arm from the joint. The henchmen was ready and wasted no time to burn the wound close.

"Wait! No more aghhhh! Ahhh!" Luke cried uncontrollably.

Faith stepped back and looked at the nurse she walked over to Luke and checked his pulse and heart rate.

"He's fine but yeah, we are going have to hook this one up to a heart monitor and blood pressure machine when you're done." The nurse said and stepped back.

"Why are you doing this? Please stop! I can't take anymore. I can't take it." Luke cried and his voice quivered.

The pain was more than he could bare and worse than anything he felt. But his tears brought him no sympathy from Faith as she swung again chopping off his left leg from the joint.

"Agh! God help me! Please help me! Someone save me! Stop this!" Luke said looking at the nurse in the room then the henchman as he placed the hot machete on his wound, burning it close.

Luke's body shook and buckled as he tried to get free. But couldn't.

Faith swung again, this time the whole leg didn't come off. It was still attached by some meat and skin.

"Sorry about that. My mind was somewhere else. I got real good at this over the years," Faith said and swung again chopping his right leg completely off from the joint.

The henchman burnt it and Luke passed out from the pain.

"I swear the men are pussy, all of them. They can dish it out but never take it. I did all of this to my mother. She didn't pass out not once. But everyone time I do this to a man he always faints like a little girl," Faith said shaking her head then passed her hatchet to one of the

henchmen, then squeezed Luke cheeks, opened his mouth and grabbed his tongue, in one swift move she sliced it out of his mouth. The new found pain woke Luke up.

"Ahhhh!" He screamed as blood and saliva poured out his mouth.

"Hold on buddy, just hold on. I'm almost there, I'll be done in one second," Faith said as a henchmen passed her an ice pick and she grab Luke by the chin.

"Ahhh! Stop," Luke tried to said as he wiggled around his arm and legs, well where they use to be at.

Faith carefully stuck the ice pick into his left earlobe until she felt a pop of his eardrum and blood and wax leaked out of his ear.

"I normally just do one ear, but I really don't like you. You killed Raven so my voice will be the last thing you ever hear," Faith said as she jammed the ice pick in his right ear and popped his eardrum.

"All done." Faith said then looked at the nurse.

"Pump him full off antibiotics and take care of his wounds if he dies you die. Oh, yeah no pain medication. I want him to feel everything, if the heart rate elevates too high give him something to put him to sleep until it drops," Faith ordered.

"Yes mistress." The nurse replied and went to work on Luke.

The henchman pushed in a cart with her supplies.

"Ughh! Ughh!" Flynn opened his eyes, then closed them the room he was in was white with the bright white led lights. Making his eyes hurt. He could hear what sounded like crying. His head wasn't strapped down but his body was. He couldn't move. He turned his head to see Luke. His arms was chopped off and so was his legs.

A nurse was wrapping them up.

"Stop your crying and heal good. I can't have you getting any infections," The nurse said.

"Hey you! What is going on over here!" Flynn shouted.

"Quiet down your turn coming," The nurse said.

"Luke! Luke are you okay" Flynn asked and Luke didn't answer.

"Luke! Answer me!" Flynn said.

"He can't hear you."

Flynn heard a voice say and knew it was Lefty. He came into the room in a wheelchair chair with a big great Dane dog beside him. The dog had to be one of the tallest dogs Flynn seen.

"I told you not to underestimate her, oh and your friend there is deaf now. Faith popped his eardrums," Lefty said.

"She must be soft. She left you alive, so bring it on. I'm not scared," Flynn said.

Lefty chuckled. *"You are still putting up that front. She's not going kill you stupid. You'll be part of the zoo, you won't die, the nurses and doctors are going make sure of it.*

Soft, I wish she was, after today no henchman will ever cross her again and since I saved Hope from you she decided to let me live but not without no consequences," Lefty said and raised his right hand and showed it was chopped off, then showed his right leg, that had been chopped off.

"I guess I'm really a lefty now. But I deserve worse, I deserve to be in her zoo, but lord knows I don't want that. I rather die or get eaten by hyenas. But I told Faith I don't think the zoo would be good enough for you. She agreed. She this dog here, this is Brock. Black ice saved him. Brock is what you'll call an evil ass pet. He has a problem with raping his owners. So after the hell, from all your limps being chop off.

You're going be out in a room with Brock here. Brock got a string sex drive.

You won't be able to run or crawl really, you'll have no arms and legs but Faith put these style of buckets on your limbs so you can move around. Walk on all fours. Brock here is going to rape you every day for a long time," Lefty said then Flynn looked at Brock staring at him and licking his lips, then he looked down to see Brock penis starting to grow hard, it look like a normal human dick.

"Hell no! Fuck no!" Flynn said as Faith entered the room.

She looked at Lefty, he lowered his head and rolled out of the room in his wheelchair.

"I see you met Brock and Lefty told you the plan. Let's get started,"

"No! Please," Flynn screamed as Faith chopped off his right leg from the joints.

"The wild hyenas are going to love eating your legs. It's like chicken wings to them," Faith said as the henchmen burnt Flynn leg.

"I'm going kill all you anointed fuckers, and get back my son and little brother Mike. I promise I'm going rejoice in your screams of pain," Faith said.

"Fuck you! Fuck you bitch!" Flynn shouted as Faith chopped off his next leg, then chopped off his arm real fast.

She step back and let her henchman burn Flynn wounds close.

"Ughhh! Ahhh!" Flynn screamed and cried louder than a new born child.

His body trembled as Faith chopped off his left arm, then waited for the henchmen to burn it close and stop the bleeding.

"God help! Help me! Lord! Help me please!" Flynn cried as Faith squeezed his cheeks and grabbed his tongue.

"God is not here, just the devil's daughter!" Faith said as she sliced his tongue off.

THE DAUGHTER OF BLACK ICE 6.

Made in United States
North Haven, CT
05 August 2022

22276810R00173